CHIMERA

CHIMERA

CHINAZA EZIAGHIGHALA

NOSETOUCH PRESS

CHICAGO • PITTSBURGH

CHIMERA

ISBN-13: 978-1-944286-37-8
Paperback Edition

Published by Nosetouch Press
www.nosetouchpress.com

For more information, contact Nosetouch Press:
info@nosetouchpress.com

Cataloging-in-Publication Data

Names: Eziaghighala, Chinaza, author.
Title: Chimera
Description: Chicago, IL : Nosetouch Press [2024]
Identifiers: ISBN: 9781944286378 (paperback)
Subjects: LCSH: Horror tales—Fiction. |
Occult—Fiction. | Paranormal—Fiction. |
GSAFD: Horror fiction. | BISAC: FICTION / Horror |
FICTION / Occult & Supernatural.

Cover & Interior Designed by Christine M. Scott
www.clevercrow.com

To Mama Rose Ofojua.
Rest well.

Chapter One

AMAKA

The crowded Mushin Road was chaotic. Women gathered in the streets hawking various items of trade while the men were mostly meat sellers or bus drivers. Yellow commercial buses were parked in the various street corners that were interspersed with dingy roads. The conductor's voice bellowed from an unseen boom box, "Ojuelegba! College gate! Yaba!" All mingled together in a strangely uniform harmony guiding people into the vehicles of their destinations.

The moist air shimmered with the wetness of rainfall, but this did not stop the buzz of the busy marketplace. I had no umbrella with me, so I knew that life would not be easy today, but to march onward, I reminded myself about how the choicest goods were in the innermost parts of the market.

My flip-flops were ruined again on my way to buy meat from a vendor. I barely escaped a huge gash on my second toe as my left foot got caught in a ditch, my body barely missing a muddy gutter bath. I was walking in my usual *clumsy manner,* as Mama would say if she were beside me, laughing mockingly at my gait.

"Stop walking like an ostrich, *Nne,*" she would say after her laughter as she walked behind me. Other times she would matter-of-factly say that "slouching does not befit a lady," before showing me her stern back. As though she derived some joy in being a figurine of sorts. Well, I definitely did not.

The Mushin meat vendors closer to the road preyed on the naïve and unsuspecting, raising prices three to four times their original. But in the inner parts, one could get things at a cost near half the original if one knew their way. I dragged my, now mangled, foot while clinging to what was left of my damaged flipflops, asking passers-by for directions to the nearest cobbler. One, in particular, reminded me of Ozioma. His yellow teeth, much like hers, glistened as he doled out directions.

"Aunty go left, follow Animashaun street, after the fourth house, count one, two, three, four houses, turn right then come out for Anifowoshe road beside the Mobil filling station. *You go find the guy there, him be correct shoemaker.*"

A shop owner beside him shook her head in wonder, and then looked at me with pity.

"How she go take know all this talk wey you talk now?"

She beckoned to me, called one of her sales girls, and after speaking some Yoruba, I could not comprehend to her, said, "Don't worry, my girl should take you to the one that is just beside this street." I muttered my thanks and hoped to God that the cobbler was really on the next street. As I followed the young girl, who was no more than sixteen, towards the cobbler, I noticed her back was arched in a way that made her buttocks protrude unnaturally. And even though I was sure there was at least a solid six-year gap between us, the girl's breasts were fuller than mine.

The crowd of sellers vying to shove their wares, pants and bras, skirts, tops, gowns, all for ridiculous prices, in my face increased as we moved further.

"What do you want, ma? I have shoes, bags, and accessories for sale."

"I have new pant and bra for you, exactly your size."

"Your tops your gowns, I have everything here."

"Stop putting those things in my face! If I want your wares, I will buy," I snapped.

"She no wan buy cloth, I dey take am go shoemaker," the young girl said.

"Abeg relax, make I sell my market," one of the Vendors said. I couldn't believe it. These people didn't seem to understand that my feet were covered in grime. I stormed out and ran as fast as my legs could carry me. I heard *"were"* which in English means madness or mad person and briefly wondered who had said it—the young girl or one of the vendors.

By the time I had gained enough distance, it didn't matter because I eventually caught sight of the cobbler. In different circumstances, I would have asked for the price before service, but the price had far less value to me than the potential athlete's foot I would have after this.

The building where the cobbler stayed was beside an abandoned one. It was all those kinds of uncompleted buildings that made you wonder if the owners were just dead or if they had run out of money to continue building. While the cobbler worked, I wondered how the green-blue algae creeping on the walls had formed and how many years of rain and sunshine had beaten it down to its current state. The cobbler looked at how I watched the building and must have thought that I was losing my mind because his lips turned up in amusement—so subtle that I could have missed it had I not been paying attention. He finished in no time, handed me my flip-flops and we made no bargain. I just paid what he asked for.

My driving slowed as I approached the gate where two security guards greeted me warmly. An albino reddened by the hot sun and a dark-skinned "Dudu" male. I searched for my gate pass and handed it over to them. Mr. Dudu quickly assessed the pass and frowned.

"Madam, this one na for the other gate," he said. Shit.

I knew I must have left something in that market after all that drama.

"Sorry sir, please it won't happen again," I said.

He came closer, leaned into my side-window and smiled at me. I knew that smile, guards used it all the time, so I was not surprised when I heard the accompanying words:

"Arrange for your boys' ma. You know that we are not allowed to let you in, but just give us something that will make this easier for us."

"We've not eaten since morning," said Albino. I handed them two five-hundred-naira notes each without further delay.

"Mama!" said Mr. Dudu, he did an exaggerated attention salute as he gestured to Albino to let me pass. As soon as I entered the compound, the rains began.

The tumbledown roads paved the way to my hostel, each turn laced with bumps. I drove while watching people run for shelter. My phone alarm went off and the screen glowed with a notification from Yetunde:

WHERE ARE YOU?

Yetunde was the closest thing I had to a friend. She had a way of handling people that I had never seen before. Maybe it was her big brown eyes and welcoming demeanour. I told her that I had a theory about her being a witch and she laughed and said that it is why I follow her around; I must be bewitched.

Two years ago, when we were freshers at the university, she had come late for lectures and just waltzed in like she owned the place. The lecturer was no lover of latecomers so he asked her to step out of the class as soon as she was caught. Yetunde walked straight towards him and they both engaged in some silent conversation no one else could hear. After close to two minutes of "yes," "nos" and "leave my classes," a smiling Yetunde walked straight into the classroom and took a seat in the front, right beside me. It was like a miracle. We did not become friends however till much later when she got diagnosed with depression last year, and we have been inseparable ever since.

During our friendship, I discovered that Yetunde lived alone in Nigeria and her parents were in the United States of America. She owned a flat of her own but chose to live in school instead. She owned a Benz but preferred to walk or ride with me. Her parents sent money from time to time to compensate for being absent. When I asked her how she was able to just take care of herself, being in Nigeria alone, she shrugged.

"I can take care of myself," she said. Sometimes, I thought that she was depressed and had to see her secret shrink because she had to go through most things by herself. We stayed in different hostels for a myriad of reasons, mine being that I did not want us to seem needy and unhealthy and hers that she needed a much larger room and air where she could smoke.

Yetunde was right on time, which was a strange but most welcome thing. She was standing beside the porter's lodge of Cooperative hostel. She seemed so unbothered by the rain and she smiled when she saw me, her white teeth glistened against dark gums, a knowing smile.

"You can like to form efficient," she said as she walked towards the car. She had a sweater, Jergens and flip-flops on. An outfit that best suited the weather.

"You cannot just try and be lazy for once, always coming early as if someone will pay you for your diligence."

"What does that mean?" I asked, in play-pretense.

"It does not matter; you don't learn because you don't listen," she said, more like laughed.

"Bad things? No."

I quickly opened the door from the inside and let her in. She was wet but didn't look like she cared much about it. She turned in her seat and looked at me.

"It is when you came that the rains decided to stop," she smiled.

I had not noticed it earlier, but the clouds were clearing. The rains had stopped and there was a shy ray of sunlight that made its way onto the windscreen.

"Play me, Laura Daigle," she said.

We both smiled as I ceded to her request. I knew Yetunde would never ask me why I wore flip-flops because she, too, had flip-flops on and didn't care who saw her. We headed to our favourite bar just outside school, it was a beer parlour around Ishaga Road where they sold pepper soup to die for. A place called Efa. We liked to go there to celebrate special days. Special days for us could mean days when Yetunde smoked less than one blunt in a month, or when I did not go out with a different guy in one month.

"I have news," she said, excited. I was not ready to feed into her energy, but she batted her lashes and pouted in such a cute way that I caved. We had ordered our usual: one plate of five-hundred-naira fish and goat meat pepper soup, and one stout for her while I had a bottle of Eva water.

"You always have news."

"This time, it's good, really good," she said.

"That's what you said the last time," I replied. Last time Yetunde had said she had good news, she hyped me up so terribly only to scream about some latest album by some Nigerian musician I cared less about.

"Don't be a spoilsport."

Her expression immediately turned sour but returned to its initial fervour just as quickly. "His name is Inyene."

It was unusual for Yetunde to talk about her male adventures, which made this particularly interesting.

"Why aren't you saying anything?"

"Am I supposed to say anything?"

"Well, you are my friend, you tell me."

"I don't want to make this awkward," I said. She looked at me and began to giggle, her hands covering her mouth showed off the black bracelet that dangled from her wrist. I always thought the bracelet she wore was too big but she had said it was a gift from a friend and knowing Yetunde, she never threw away gifts. The flip-flops she wore were my gifts to her one day when she had no footwear to wear out. I will cherish this gift, she had said. I found it strange but endearing how she loved the simple things.

"You already are! Just ask me your questions already," she said.

Yetunde's nose crinkled whenever she mentioned Q-words, it was like a weird allergic reaction she was not acutely aware of that made it all the more adorable because of her default defiant expression. I wondered what questions she expected me to ask. *Does he make you happy? Do you guys have sex? Is sex good?* I only felt the pressure and couldn't think.

"I don't know what to say."

"Say that you are happy for me."

"I am happy for you."

"Not so robotic, with feeling," she quipped.

She looked at me, her eyes searching mine for hope or encouragement or both and at that moment, I realized that my friend wanted this. I was truly happy for her. I stood up and went to her, pulled her close to me in the tightest embrace I could muster, and whispered in her ear "I am happy you are happy." When I released her, she screamed in excitement. She was really happy and this meant I would be happy, too.

"Let's take a selfie," she said. She brought out her phone and I feigned a smile as she took our pictures.

I came down with malaria during the weekend, when Yetunde was staying with Inyene, so I went home. Home smelt of shea butter. The oily, stuffed scent was neither appealing nor repulsive. The best way to tell I was home was hearing Mama's nagging about my adopted sister, Ozioma. She usually began with how Ozioma did not put in the right breed of fish that she had asked her to put into the pot of soup and eventually it always led to how Ozioma would be the death of her, and how Ozioma hated her.

When Mama realized I was sick, her instincts kicked in. She laid out the bed for me and removed my clothing. She asked if I would bathe myself or rather have her do it for me. I chose the former because she seemed not to understand how odd it was for me to be naked before her. She assigned Ozioma with the task of picking up my plates later while she fanned me and prayed for me to sleep.

Mama would come in from time to time and ask me how I felt if I needed more food and my answer was always no, I felt my phone vibrate in my pocket and brought it out. The LED screen showed a text from Yetunde:

Get well soon, will come to see you.

I knew she had heard of my illness because of what happened in school that morning. I was giving a presentation on human papillomavirus with the rest of my classmates when words began to fail me. The lecturer had thought that my incoherence was due to my ineptitude. I had no time during the week to go to the Staff clinic even when I started vomiting and stooling. That morning, I had intended to get through with my part quickly, so I started the presentation in haste. But upon starting, I felt my head begin to explode and the last thing I remember was the lecturer's look of disgust. When I woke up in the Accident and Emergency room, I was told that I had malaria and it was getting serious but I could stay in the hospital or get treated at home. I chose home with my chest.

Mama walked into my room very late at night and I felt her place her hand on my neck as if checking my temperature. She paced up and down the room, closed the open windows and curtains before covering me with a blanket. She sat down on a plastic chair that was beside my bed and watched me as I went back to sleep. By morning, Mama called for prayers as was our custom. After prayers, she talked about the importance of one having a relationship with God and left for whatever August or town hall meeting she found interesting. She dragged Ozioma with her, of course.

Later that morning, the house was empty and I was alone with my thoughts. I turned on the TV, but sleep had other plans. As I started to nod off, I could swear that I saw a silhouette standing beside the television and walking toward me but the knock on the living room door startled me awake and I assumed what I saw was a dream. The incessant knocks continued and with as much strength as I could muster, I took weary steps down the stairs, opened the door slowly without asking who it was, expecting Yetunde, because she was the only person I knew with such horrible knocking habits, yet Inyene's tall frame stood before me. His OUD cologne reached my nostrils before I could look at his face. He was not much taller than I, with his flat nose and ugly brown hair that looked like the fur of a sewer rat, and he had the same figure with the silhouette in my dreams. He looked like he was lost for a moment, hands in his pockets full of cool, then as if remembering to speak, he blurted, "Hi."

Chapter Two

INYENE

Walking to class had never been my thing, but running was the icing on the cake. Ahmed was about four solid strides behind me. I could hear my feet hit the pavements, hard, one after the other, my legs carried me and brought me closer and closer to what I wanted. The weather was perfect for speed, humid enough to cool, and dry enough to withstand rain. My breathing was less laboured than Ahmed's, as the cool wind kissed my face, I could feel the pride in my heart when I knew for certain I would win, yet again. Ahmed's heavy footsteps suddenly stopped.

Keep your focus, don't look behind, I thought. Then I stopped cold in my tracks, my momentum propelling me forward as I stumbled and almost fell.

"What is wrong with you?" I snapped. We were already late enough as it was, stopping at the entrance of the outpatient clinic was not the best way to make sure that we wouldn't be caught coming in late.

"I am tired, I no do again."

Ahmed looked funny, his dark skin was drenched in sweat, he looked like he would faint soon. The only thing supporting his body was the car parked beside him. Reaching for his pocket, he brought out his inhaler and took three puffs.

"But when you wanted to eat and I said we would be late, you said you would run, and we haven't even tried at all but you've given up. We'll be late for sure," I said.

He knew that we needed to sign our logbooks today and he still decided to do this, I was exasperated. I knew this was going to happen because it had happened before, much earlier in the year, we had both agreed to run together in the mornings and evenings to keep fit but Ahmed had brought his car the next morning and told me that he would follow me and cheer me on. Now our potential futures actually depended on how soon we could get to the wards but he was lagging behind like the couch potato that he was.

"We are late already; I am not moving an inch," he replied and true to his word, he leaned on the car for support.

I looked at Ahmed, rivulets of sweat dripping from his forehead. His clinical coat was nearly drenched and said, "Oya, let's walk."

By the time we reached the wards, ward rounds were nearly over. The pink-coloured walls painted with superheroes or cartoon characters looked like a bad attempt at an American children's ward at best, but the angry-looking nurses reminded us of our true location. When I looked closer, I noticed that the Superman caricature—once a vibrant blue and red painting—was now faded and the white ceiling was peeled, each peel wound up like a cinnamon roll. So much for the attempt to beautify everything. Each section of the ward housed a variety of specific cases. There was an area for heart cases, kidney cases, gastrointestinal cases and more of such subspecialty cases. I could see my unit up ahead, a group of about twenty people wearing white coats huddled together with a handsome woman wearing a suit standing in the centre. Ahmed and I slid into the group unnoticed by the woman, Dr. Ajayi, our consultant, my guardian.

"You could have done better!" she said.

The nurses looked at her and each other but remained silent. Everyone was quiet, as if at some solemn funeral.

"We can't keep losing patients like this. This country is messed up, but we have to try harder," she continued.

There was a child, not more than five years old lying on the bed, looking lifeless and pale, one of the nurses was giving him chest compressions, even though he looked dead already. A doctor from the managing team was beside her with an AMBU bag, ready to give the required breaths after compressions. Each pump on the chest made the child's ribs flare. The nurse handed over to the managing doctor once he tired.

"What time is it?" said Dr. Ajayi

No matter how many times I experienced this, it was always the same sad and empty feeling. From the corner of my eye, I could see a man dressed in faded Ankara holding onto himself beside the bed, he stifled his cries and sank unto the floor. Dr. Ajayi reached out to the man who in turn refused her hand.

"Ayọ, ji, irawọ mi o ko le fi mi silẹ bayi, o le ṣe abojuto ara mi ati iya rẹ nikan, iwọ ko le yan iku."

Ayo, wake up, my star you cannot leave me like this, you can only take care of myself and your mother, you cannot choose death.

"E pele, sir. You need to get your house in order. If you cry, how do you expect your wife to react?" Dr. Ajayi said.

The man could take it no more, he wailed and wailed and rolled on the hospital floor. I did not pity him, not because I had no capacity for pity, but because I was tired of having to re-live this repeatedly. We all knew that the cause of death could have been something easily prevented if brought to the hospital on time, but could you blame patients when healthcare can be so unaffordable? I found out that the boy had sickle cell disease, and was having a crisis—acute chest syndrome. He had background attention deficit hyperactivity disorder. Dr. Ajayi was here because she had therapy sessions with him, and she wanted to sign him off. He had autism as well or something of that peculiar nature. All the other doctors had gone off to sign the paperwork, but she had stayed back to help the father cope with his grief. I didn't know how she had the capacity for such human suffering. I knew, however, that I was not so patient.

Dr. Ajayi ended the ward round early and began signing our logbooks. I waited in line in front of Ahmed and when it was my turn she smiled.

"You still come to school, Inyene," she joked.

"Yes, ma," I said.

Ever since my parents died, I had been taking care of myself and moving things along, until I met her. Dr. Ajayi was a blessing to me from our very first meeting when she decided that she would double as my guardian. She had asked me what I wanted to become.

"A doctor," I had said.

"Why not consider psychiatry?" she asked.

I didn't take her seriously. I didn't see myself as a shrink like her; she was pretty awesome at listening to people and I lack that kind of patience and time when money needed to be made.

"Did you see how I broke the bad news?" she asked, drawing me back to my present reality.

I paused before answering, sure that she would catch me in my lies.

"You created rapport?"

She laughed and returned my logbook. When she was done, I patiently waited for my friend.

"All these things are bad omens and signs. A child dying at the beginning of a new month is not a good thing." Gozie spoke up as we left the ward in silence. Gozie usually had the most superstitious reasons for everything. Once, he said that he believed a prayer that was said on him was what healed an injury he had incurred despite going to the hospital first. I didn't understand why he reasoned the way he did, or how he got into medical school in the first place. He was lucky he had good looks to cover up for what a dud he could be sometimes.

"What is the point of bringing patients if they will only die?" I asked.

"The point is that they tried," Ahmed said.

"It's just sad," I said. Gozie nodded. Ahmed furrowed his brows as if deep in thought.

Ahmed always thought that these things were what they were and what you saw was all there was. I envied that, how he always knew just what to say and how to say it reasonably.

"Abeg, wetin we fit do this weekend?" Ahmed asked. "How far you now Inyene?"

"No mind Inyene, *na babe im go follow na,*" Gozie said.

"*Na you sabi,*" I said.

I had nothing to say to them. I just wanted to live my life as I would like. I had no serious plans for the weekend, I just wanted to go with the flow or at least flow as it went.

Two ladies approached us dressed informally for clinical classes so it was safe to assume they were in basic medical classes. The one on the left was the vivacious Yetunde. We all knew her. Those who didn't know her at least heard about her. She was a sister, a brother, a sure babe. The one on the right I had never seen before. She was a plain Jane and looked less confident compared to her friend. Her hair was shaved low while Yetunde had a full mane of natural hair. Her ears were without earrings, too. A picture that portrayed her as a rebel.

"Hi, Ahmed and you are?" Yetunde quizzed.

Her eyes fell to me. Thankfully I looked away from her friend fast enough to not be considered a weirdo.

"Inyene, don't you know me? We've met before," I said.

"I don't remember. What kind of name is Inyene?"

Yetunde's friend remained silent as she continued her questioning.

"An indigenous name."

Her friend signaled to her, but she continued speaking in her shrill voice, "Okay, indigenous person, I'm Yetunde."

She stopped talking as if waiting for me to respond when I had already responded and she smiled and held her hand out for a shake.

"So, what's up now?" said Ahmed. I quickly let her hand go.

According to Ahmed, Yetunde was his self-appointed school daughter. I wondered if they commit incest because she couldn't be my school daughter and it could remain platonic.

"I want that Robbins and Cotran hard copy."

"But I thought you said you preferred the soft copy?"

Ahmed led Yetunde to a corner a few steps away leaving Yetunde's friend, Gozie, and I all by ourselves.

Her friend had stayed mute, her eyes searching the floor. Her nails were bitten down to the bud, she shifted unsteadily from one leg to the next, fidgeting with her trouser pockets and handbag.

"I'll be leaving now," Gozie said. "Lots to prep for and I'm on call this night, *abeg* help me tell Ahmed."

"No *wahala,* take care," I said. Glad he was leaving me and the lady alone.

"So, what's up?" I asked.

"Who were you talking to?" she replied.

"Amaka, let's go, Ahmed thank you so much," Yetunde appeared suddenly, grabbing her friend by the arm while flashing me an inviting look. Her steps were measured and precise, the view from behind was like nothing I had ever seen. Ahmed slapped the back of my head at that moment, something I didn't deserve.

***

Efa bar was dimly lit. The cool sounds jived in the background, suiting the open ground where the bar stood. Ahmed had gotten us some Arizona from one of the dealers, he sat down across from me and tore out the rizla. Skillfully, he poured out the weed into his palm and mashed it. It reminded me of how the local woman mashed pepper using her smooth rock anytime we came to the bar, with utter concentration and stealth. He poured the mashed *grass* into the paper in a straight line and carefully held one end of the paper which he steadily swished and turned till it began to form a roll that extended to the other end. He then used his second hand for support to align and properly distribute the weight of the grass, forming a ballpoint shape. He rolled the tail end of the joint and passed it to me. I lit the smoke and passed it to Gozie, who passed it back to me and I passed it on to Ahmed and it went on and on until we exhausted it. This ritual of ours always seemed sacred, with the joint roller as the priest while we served as members of the congregation waiting to share in holy communion. Ahmed left me alone when he found his girl. She was dark and laughed so loud that I could hear her from my seat. I recognized her from school and waved, she waved back and smiled.

"I dey come," he said.

"No problem," I said. I eyed the girl from where I sat and she seemed clean. His choices in women seemed to improve over time.

I remained seated on the chair and focused on the football match playing on the television. Languidly holding my beer in hand, I vibed to the music around and everything began to blur. The bar girl came over to ask if I needed more drinks and I told her to bring more beer. I saw several classmates and schoolmates. A sight that was not odd because our school wasn't a big one, everyone knew everyone. From the corner of my eye, I caught sight of Amaka, she was huddled in a corner of the bar, away from everyone.

"No be Amaka be that?" Gozie asked, having come into awareness of her presence, too.

"It looks like her," I said. Then I thought that if she was here then her friend may be as well so I searched around to be doubly sure that she wasn't.

"You should talk to her," he said. I wanted to so I got up and walked straight at her, keeping it as steady as I could manage.

She was seated alone in a corner, relaxed as if she owned the place. The smoke she exhaled formed a sort of boundary around her like some form of protection to ward of predators like me.

"Excuse me, ma'am, may I join you?"

Her eyes turned to me, surprise and fear flashing across her face in an instant before it returned to normal.

"Is that how they creep up on you in your village?" she retorted. She sounded tired.

"I'm sorry if I scared you."

"You did not, I just need space is all."

"Bad day?"

Her features began to relax as if the statement was a trigger. Her head bowed, in concentration, as she tried to light her joint. I reached for my lighter to help her.

"Sort of." I lit it up and she took a long drag.

"Ahhh, that's the stuff," she said.

"Wanna talk about it?" I asked.

She looked at me and smiled, a crooked smile. She was inviting me; I knew how this worked and I knew that she wanted me.

"Here, try it."

She offered me her smoke and I took a drag. Beautiful. The blast completely engulfed my senses. I could see the colours grow like a rainbow before my eyes and when it reached a crescendo, explode and go back to the dip of chill. It was not like any other weed I had ever smoked.

"This stuff is good," I said.

"I know, right," she said.

"Where did you get it?"

"I could tell you, but it's not legal."

I don't know why I felt she was right. I didn't press further. We both silently took turns until we finished it. As she was about to stand up, I held her hand.

"Leaving so soon?" I asked.

She stopped and looked at me as if to challenge why I held her hand. Looking at her, I noticed that she was pretty hot. She had pretty eyes. She didn't look as withdrawn as I remembered either, rather she looked alive and on fire like the colours in my eyes.

"I know what you are doing," she said.

"Really, what am I doing?"

"Looking for a way to get me to like you."

"Wow, caught."

She laughed, her laugh sounded genuine and sweet as it echoed in my ears. I didn't want to be alone this night so I pressed on. I stood up.

"You should not be staying here by yourself."

"Do you have a better suggestion?" she asked.

Her eyes bored into mine as I stood and held out my hand to her. She pulled herself up. We walked in silence, heading deeper into the surrounding streets.

~~~~~~~~~

The morning light filled the hotel room and woke me. Yetunde stood beside the curtains, wearing my shirt, she was aglow, a spring in her step.

"Good morning," she smiled, a smile so wide I was sure if she smiled any further, her lips would rip apart. I stood up from the bed and began to dress.

"That was fun, wasn't it?" she continued.

I had not fully understood what happened, because what I last remembered was booze, weed, colours, and a blasted headache. When I saw Yetunde instead of Amaka I knew it had happened again even though I didn't intend for it to happen this way. Trying to ignore her presence in the room as I sieved
~~~~~~~~~

through my memories. I wish I could explain to Yetunde what just happened because I, too, didn't seem to understand what just happened. I had only skipped about a week's dose which wasn't that much in my opinion, therefore, I didn't expect this to happen, not so soon anyway.

"Are you okay?" She faced me now.

"I'm fine," I said, curtly. I already breached the rules, skipped my meds, and fucked up in a colossal way.

"I've got to get to school," she said. School! I jumped as fast as I could as she watched me make a fool of myself and dress up like someone doing a bad choreography.

"Yetunde."

"Yes?"

"This never happened, it was a mistake, right?"

She walked toward me as if drunk, unsure what I was saying, "I don't understand why you are making this such a big deal."

I wish I could just tell her "I'm making this a big deal because it is a big deal and I kind of just person swapped you," but I couldn't; so, instead, I just said, "Let's go."

She stood up and followed me as we made our way out of the hotel.

"You did what?" Ahmed was seated on his water-bed-couch thing that looked like it was about to swallow him whole so when he spoke, he sank deeper into it and looked like he would have a hard time coming out. I had come straight to him because classes were cancelled. His eyes darted everywhere before he replied to me.

"I warned you that Yetunde is a bit delicate."

I know he warned me. I had understood the warning and warned myself about the warning, too. I just made a mistake. I wish it didn't happen. I wish I took my drugs.

"How?"

He stood up and moved to the window, thinking carefully before he spoke. His new girlfriend's picture was his phone wallpaper. She was dark and beautiful; it was hard to ignore. Her name was Demola. She was the girl he had spoken to at the bar the other night and he had been asking her out for a while. They had gone on a couple of dates but the answer had always been no and now it was yes because he had made her his wallpaper.

"Yetunde is just delicate and this," he motioned to my body like I was some decrepit thing, something lost and unforgivable. I had not looked at myself in a while but I understood what exactly he was saying. I just wished I had a better way of explaining without sounding like I was making excuses.

"No problem." I didn't need an elaboration, it's not like I liked her, all this was a simple mistake that would blow over.

"I'm sorry about this, man," I say this with as much truth as I can muster. His back was turned on me now, but that could not hide the disappointment in his sagged shoulders.

"You know she is suffering from depression, right?"

I had no idea. She did not look like it at all. She looked happy and full of life to me.

"She is being managed for it right now and I don't know if she is stable enough to just be playing around, though," he continued.

I understood. Moving forward, Yetunde was to be left alone.

Eyeing the new wallpaper, I blurted. "This your babe fine, *sha*."

The girl had a big smile plastered on her face. She was tall and fit with dark hair. Her eyes glistened with promise. A promise of happiness.

He seemed to take the words in as if he had a lot to say. It seemed like a lot of growth on his part because dating girls was never our thing. We usually just hooked up or had arrangements.

"Yeah, she asked me to do that though, put up her picture as my wallpaper. It's weird but I'm like 'okay, she wants it so do it,'" he spoke while eyeing the floor. I could not be more elated, I didn't know when I had started laughing, he soon joined me.

"Congrats, man."

He smiled, and for a brief second, he frowned as well, maybe he realised what he was doing now, he was fulfilling a commitment, or was at least trying. I couldn't help but be happy for him.

"I go sha tell am say you dey follow babe upandan," I said.

He looked at me and made as if to hit the back of my head, I dodged it and his hand hung mid-air. Then I suddenly felt a punch in my gut.

"Where is that, your Xbox?" I asked.

We sat down on his plain moth-eaten couch and settled into a game that involved us shooting at and killing make-believe people. My thoughts wandered to Yetunde's friend, Amaka. Her black skin and pink lips began to fill my thoughts.

Chapter Three

AMAKA

There was no light at home and all our phones were dead. I used to have a power bank, but Ozioma had ruined it last week when she was having one of her legendary tussles with Mama. We were at the mercy of the PHCN, the company that supplied electricity, and most times, they hardly came through.

We, three, all sat down on my bed laughing and telling jokes. I was exhausted, but luckily Mama had returned and prepared food for Inyene and Yetunde. She brought in a steaming plate of Oha soup and Semolina, I noticed Yetunde's eyes light up when she saw the food. She should have come to the world as Igbo, with the way she ate Igbo food, or maybe just food in general.

"Oh my God! Oha!" she said. Inyene declined the food, mentioning something about having eaten earlier.

"So, you will not eat the food I went great lengths to make for you, my son?" Mama said. Her caramel skin laced with hypopigmented patches made her seem so frail.

"Oh, Mama! Okay Ma, I will eat." He dug into the food as Mama watched, smiling to herself.

His muscles were tight and firm as he rolled each morsel of food into a ball and dipped it into the soup. The food made contact with his black lips and I wished that it was my lips against his. I silently observed the both of them, Inyene seemed out of place. His smile was not so genuine, but Yetunde radiated a warmth that I had never seen before. She used every opportunity that she had to hold his hand, while he seemed to remove it every chance he got.

"So, when did you guys become a thing?" I asked, curious. Mama had gone by now, so we could have such conversations. Inyene stopped as if unsure whether to deny or assert the question, Yetunde looked like she was about to burst with an answer.

"It just happened," Inyene said. He looked like he would give that kind of response and I decided not to push further.

We played Ludo and Whot and I won every game although Inyene insisted that he let me win, but I knew better. We tried Monopoly but Yetunde didn't understand it so we had to stop.

Inyene stared at me sometimes; his longing stares when Yetunde took her toilet breaks. Sometimes he winked at me when he was making witty comments about feminism or when he told dry jokes.

I felt hot and heavy inside, a feeling I've never truly experienced before. It was a different feeling, like fire in my lungs or breathing in hot air. But sometimes it felt like urine, the strange urge to pee yet hope not to wet myself. Yetunde who had no clue. She looked so happy, and I didn't want to be that person, I didn't want to be that friend, I didn't want to be the person to spoil her happiness.

Inyene began telling us cat jokes that were not funny at all, but the confidence he had in telling them made me laugh. And when the rains began Yetunde started drifting off and I noticed.

"What's wrong?" I wrapped my arms around her as I watched her drift, staring at the skies as if something was there.

She hugged me back in a bear hug and said in an almost dreamy tone, "They won't bring the lights now, will they?"

"Yetunde, tell us that your cool story now so that we won't be bored or we can at least talk about how you and Inyene met," I said. I motioned for her to stand up while glancing at Inyene from the corner of my eye. His smile was so big, his yellow teeth laced with some small black patches that contrasted against his full dark lips. Yetunde hated talking about her relationships. Not that she had so many, she just had enough to get by. The one time she spoke about a boyfriend, I thought they would end up together but Yetunde had come back to our room with tears in her eyes and silence. We never spoke about it and I had decided to let sleeping dogs lie. However, I wanted to see if she would really share about their relationship. How they met and what exactly transpired between them but she would rather pick death than defeat.

"Fine," she replied.

I signalled to her and quickly side-eyed Inyene. He looked so bored; he was playing with his dead phone, twirling it on his index finger as if that was a surefire way to recharge it. She flashed me a look of disapproval and stood up.

"Oh, all right," she continued.

"Yay!" I said. "E for effort!"

No one really told stories for fun anymore but Yetunde and I decided that we would keep telling each other stories to remain more African and "grounded", and because we saw it in "Tales by Moonlight" a popular Nigerian television show most of us watched when we were younger. Part of our ritual was that we would research our stories and tell them under the moonlight lying side by side like they do in oyinbo movies. We decided that it would be a bonding and relaxing activity that we could do on the rooftop of her hostel because it had such a great view. That was the first time I had heard the story she was going to tell. It was always the same story with Yetunde even though we agreed that we would do the extra research and try to enhance the experience, but Yetunde, being who she was, never listened.

"Do you know the story of Bolatito and Iku?" she said. Setting the mood. She stood up from the bed and began to pace the room, dramatizing what she was saying. A full orator in her element using all of her senses to portray the sense of urgency.

Of course, we did not know—at least Inyene did not—but we sat down, pretend wide-eyed, anticipating what she had to say. She said, "Bolatito was a princess in the olden days in a kingdom far far away. She was so beautiful, that she was seen as the fairest among maidens. Iku, the God of the Dead, saw her and felt well pleased with her, he wanted her for himself, so he struck a deal with her father, immortal life for his daughter as long as she belonged to him."

She paced up and down the room, voicing the characters of Iku and Bolatito, making a show of her small story. She deepened her voice when talking about Iku and lightened it when she spoke about Bolatito. She continued...

"Unknown to him, Bolatito already fell in love with a hunter in the village. She got pregnant for him out of wedlock and gave birth to the baby in exile. Bolatito's father arranged for the child to be sent off to another village for some time, and when the time came for the agreed payment, Bolatito's father tricked Iku by taking away his calabash of coins, where spirits put money before entering into the afterlife. Iku was so enraged, that he killed Bolatito as vengeance, taking her spirit into his world and sending her back to the human world every fifty years so she can be sacrificed to him because she belonged to him. The End."

Inyene clapped so loudly, I almost could not hear myself think.

"That was fantastic, I never knew you had a flair for stories," he said, his grin was strained.

"My mom knew a thing or two, a family trait of sorts. The real story ends with the God of Death eating Bolatito's body parts, but that is just very disturbing and isn't a great ending," Yetunde replied. There was a riotous noise in the area as people screamed UP NEPA! Electricity was back and the fan revved slowly, then faster as we all rushed to charge our phones and focus on social media.

We ended the day listening to music. Yetunde took the dishes to the kitchen and I was left with Inyene. He put on his earphones to listen to music despite the already booming speaker in the background. We were silent for a bit. I could hear the background music playing from his phone. I wondered if he could hear me, but he didn't seem like he was interested in talking. I stood up to clear the games we had played when he spoke up.

"Thanks for the food; your grandmother can cook."

"You are welcome," I replied. "Do you mean that or are you being sarcastic again?"

"Why would you think I was being sarcastic?" he asked with a smirk.

"Never mind," I said. He was fully aware of what I meant. Yetunde was a very bad storyteller, yet he applauded her skills like some delirious fan meeting his idol for the first time. He stood up to join me as I stacked up the Ludo game board. My hands brushed his and I apologised. It was awkward but I could still feel the heat at the back of my hand as if it were still there.

"I'm sorry about that."

"You don't have to say sorry," he said. "There is nothing to be sorry about."

He collected the board and placed it on the table in my room.

"What type of music do you listen to?" he asked.

"I don't listen to music, I'm more of a reader," I replied.

He removed one of his earphones and gave them to me. I listened to the song with him. It was Fela Kuti's *Water.*

"Isn't this old?" I asked.

"Yeah. It is, but the message is forever young," he said.

I sat down with him and listened to music. We both moved silently to beat, then I rested my head on his shoulders, and he didn't stop me. I felt his hand slide to my lower back and hold there.

"You guys, I need to go," Yetunde screamed.

We both quickly separated as she walked into the room. She made straight for Inyene and dragged him to his feet.

"Chill now, I'm coming already," he said.

"We need to go now, I have that appointment with my psychiatrist and I don't want to be late," she said.

"I love you, babes," she said. "Thanks for hosting me and my man."

She squeezed his arm as she said this and I felt a pain in my chest. She was about to leave when she stopped in her tracks and brought out her phone.

"Oh no, Yetunde, I'm not in the mood," I said, but I was too late. She was pouting and pleading with puppy dog eyes and I couldn't say no. We all huddled together and took a picture then she made a quick video introducing all of us that ended with her saying, "Thanks, guys, for hanging out with my friends."

Inyene and Yetunde left that evening, I watched them as they walked out of the gate. It was obvious Inyene did not like her as much as she liked him. I only hoped for that to change over time, but a part of me wanted him to like her less.

Chapter Four

INYENE

~~~

I was running again. I could hear my laboured breathing as I tried my best to run faster than the fastest I had ever run. It was like breaking the sound barrier in a superhero movie, only this time, there were no powers and time was of the essence. It was nearing evening and I could hear the noises of the traffic jam outside the school gate. I navigated my way through the school cafeteria, nearly bumping into someone with food.

"Sorry!" I screamed.

Passersby across the road watched me, some gestured towards me with upturned noses and bewildered looks. I didn't stop; I didn't care. My heart was racing and I could feel the creeping tiredness in my muscles as they ached from strain, but I pushed myself because I had to get there. I got to the Accident and Emergency room on time. Stopping to suck in as much air as my lungs could allow. I saw Amaka ahead, she looked so beautiful and sad. Her eyes always looked so sad. She was pacing, a bandage plastered on her wrist. She saw me and I could tell from the look in her eyes that it was worse than I anticipated.

"Where is she?" I asked. She pointed inside.

Amaka called me earlier to tell me about Yetunde. She told me that she found her pale, lying down on the bare floor of her bathroom, wrists slit. I didn't understand how Yetunde could do something like that initially because it seemed so strange that she could truly want to snuff out her light, a light that shone brightly and spread to everyone around her. I went
~~~

inside, not prepared for what I saw. The entrance of the emergency room had a certain melancholy about it, more so than even the wards. The nurses were unnecessarily rude to us as if we were the cause of their problems. Patients were in droves outside, waiting on someone to allow them to come into the building. Some had dead relatives in cars and wanted to collect death certificates or at least move them to the morgue but everything felt the same, everything felt like death and myself, Yetunde and Amaka were in the place of death.

The walls were laced with tiles and the floor was terrazzo. The nurses wore checked blue shits with plain trousers or skirts, the emergency nurses' uniform. The cleaners and maids wore plain blue and cleaned up after the patients. Flying potties, bloodstained sheets, doctors in gloves and clinical coats. Everyone was moving, actively getting things done.

Yetunde's wrists were up in bandages, she was on a rebreather mask connected to a cylinder because there was no light to turn on the oxygen that flowed through the walls. The nurses looked indifferent as they hovered over her and I understood why. She was just another one of the thousands of patients in this hospital. She was a statistic, just another number, hospital number 1156.

"She sent me a voice note, telling me she loved me but this is goodbye. I didn't understand," Amaka croaked. I looked at her bed, my mind going in a million directions. This was my fault and I felt my mind split in a thousand directions as I hoped and prayed that she would be fine.

<center>~~~~~~~~</center>

"You complete me," Yetunde said.

She was lying down with a towel wrapped around her midsection. Her face was a vision and her voice was music. We were seated in my hostel room; Ahmed was out so we had the place to ourselves for a time. The room was dimly lit with neon lights. There were a table and a chair, acouch in the middle and a bed on the floor in the far corner of the room. The flat-screen television was turned off and there were clothes flung around the floor.

"Don't say that," I said.

I was seated on the chair opposite her, blunt in hand wondering how in the world I got to this point and what I could have done to prevent all this from happening. Yetunde stood up, allowing her towel to drop as she approached me. She climbed onto my lap and cupped my face in her hands.

"Do I look like a joke to you? I mean what I am saying." She was maniacal now; I could not help but feel an overwhelming sense of guilt. Ahmed had said she was sensitive, but I didn't know the extent. The warmth of her skin and uneasiness in her eyes served to distract me. I suddenly felt queasy about this, I didn't know how best to say what had to be said. This was becoming a game I could not keep up with anymore.

"I told you, no feelings attached."

"I can't help my feelings."

"I can't help you, I'm sorry."

"Even if I am pregnant for you?"

Her words hit like shrapnel. Although I knew she had to be calling my bluff, I still felt that she had tried a very bold and audacious method even for her. She couldn't be pregnant; I mean, we only hooked up a couple of times and we used condoms. I pulled myself as far away from her as possible. The small of her nose wrinkled and I could see the pool of tears in her eyes.

"Do a pregnancy test, then we discuss," I said as I gently pushed her off me.

She got up and moved to the other side of the room. I almost felt sorry for her, but I knew this was the right thing to do. I didn't love her and it would be very unfair to her to treat her in a callous manner. She was stunning; any guy would want her; I just wasn't ready for that. Not now, not yet.

"Fine. You'll be hearing from me soon."

Those were the last words she said before she left, and I could feel my hair stand on end thinking about them. I had mulled over her statement for the whole of sixty seconds before moving on with my life, trusting that nothing could surprise me and she would not be reckless. Now, Amaka said she had donated a pint of blood but it would not be enough. I got tested and seemed to be her perfect match as well. Feeling the blood being sucked dry from my body was a new kind of high. I was oddly at peace with the whole process, yet I felt drained and wished for renewal and replacement.

Amaka and I were then asked to wait while the health workers worked—this was new territory for them, too—because no one ever tried to commit suicide in school before now. People had threatened, of course. Last year, there was a boy who had climbed the rooftops of the male hostel and made a scene shouting about how he was going to jump because he was tired of school life. He had repeated for his fourth year straight and felt that there was no need to continue. The school authorities hardly responded rapidly to these things, however, other people gathered around and tried to dissuade him. It took close to six hours to dissuade him from jumping off. That was my first experience of self-harm. I had watched from below as a mere spectator, not necessarily interested in saving the boy but admiring his courage. I watched him and imagined myself in his place. Alone on the rooftop with the winds blowing against my skin, maybe holding a blunt in hand. It would be my last blunt as I announced to the world my reasons for dying were of a mental nature, yet I knew that as my lips spoke the truth, my legs would quiver and become unsteady. My hair would be raised as I placed one foot in front of the other and I attempted to leap off the building, and despite people's voices, one voice would be clearest to me.

"Will she be okay?" Amaka asked, massaging the skin over her hand where they had just taken her blood. I didn't know why she asked me that kind of question because I didn't know the answer to such a question. I didn't know if she would be okay and I wanted to say "No, Amaka I don't know."

Instead, I blurted, "Of course now, of course," as I brought her into my embrace. I pitied Amaka; she looked so vulnerable. I wondered about Yetunde's parents and I wondered if I should call them or if I should tell Amaka to call them. I didn't think it made any sense to not keep them in the loop but Amaka had said, she would not want her parents to know, so I perished the idea. It seemed that I could only hope that Yetunde wouldn't die and we could all get back to our lives.

I was half asleep when the nurse tapped me. Amaka was curled up on my lap and I was told that it was time for patient relatives to leave. Outside, the night sky was pitch-black with the calm and sublime feel of a night with many memories, I wondered if it will remember that a woman almost died because she almost had a baby for me.

"Visiting hours are over, one of you has to leave," she said and walked away.

I watched Amaka breathing. She shivered and as my hand touched hers, I could feel its icy coldness, deprived of warmth like some cold-blooded Agama Lizard. I imagined her nodding at me as a lizard with her dull dark skin and me, with my orange hue would respond with a nod and we would nod our way into laying many eggs and burying it in the ground hoping that they become children.

"Amaka."

"Hmm," she said, waking up.

"You need to leave."

"I don't want to." She sat up and looked at me defiantly. A part of her I had never seen before.

"She is my friend and your girlfriend," she continued. "Let them come and chase me out."

"But you are freezing," I said. "It is better that I stay."

"No."

She stood up, walked to Yetunde's bedside and took the only seat beside her friend as I followed her.

"I can't just leave her; you know I can't," she said, holding Yetunde's hands in hers.

"You aren't. I am here for her." I said. "Amaka you are freezing and tired, the blood they took is taking its toll on you and you haven't eaten or slept yet. Do you want to die, too?"

"It's the same for you." She stood up abruptly and nearly collapsed. I held her just in time.

"Can you see? You can't stay tonight. Let me stay, we can take turns, you can come tomorrow."

"Promise me you will tell me if anything changes," she muttered.

"I promise."

I looked at her as she walked away. I could tell that she was processing so many things at once. She was racked with the guilt of leaving her best friend. She walked and kept glancing back until she got to the gate. Looking at her as she left the hospital crushed me, she seemed so helpless, her eyes screamed for help amidst the confusion and there was nothing that I could do.

I heard her voice, dry and shrill but audible, it woke me up and I could not unhear it. We were in the ward now. Dr. Ajayi had come earlier to the Accident and Emergency ward to transfer us to the Psych ward. I was not supposed to stay with Yetunde, but she allowed me.

"We all need friends during trying times," she had said.

I had also made a promise to Amaka and I was intent on following through. My head was banging again and the lights kept blinking, causing me to squint. Yetunde was still lying on the bed, frail and vulnerable. The oxygen mask was off now, but she looked like she was barely breathing. I strained hard to make out what she seemed to be saying, but all I heard were sighs and sniffs; she was crying. I stood up as quickly as

I could and went to her side. She looked pale and frail, she had lost the gleam in her eye and it was replaced with pleading.

"Get me out of here, please," she croaked.

That would be impossible, I thought. She was in the Psychiatry ward and they had strict rules about how patients were to be discharged. I wish she knew this, too, but I was not even sure about her current mental state.

"You can't go now, Yetunde, not until the doctors come tomorrow to see you," I replied in the best way I knew how.

On hearing what I said, she kicked her legs in the air, held bed rails with her hands and pulled herself, albeit weakly, to her feet. The drip stand fell while she struggled and I moved in to help her. I threw her arm around my neck and hoisted her up from the bed. She felt so light. Like a feather, a dainty feather.

"Help me, Inyene, I can't stay here. Please, I want to go home," she pleaded.

I called out to any of the health workers available, a nurse came to assist me. I tried laying her back down on the bed but she refused.

"I want to go home," she said again and again until it began to sound like an anthem.

I called Dr. Ajayi for help. "Give me a couple of minutes, I will send someone over." Dr. Ajayi said.

In about that amount of time, there was a House officer on the ward to help. I tried to explain how Yetunde must feel to him, but he refused.

"I can't let her go home, her tests results are not back yet, we sedated her, so it is normal for her to react in this way, please hold her while I get her medication."

"She can DAMA, can't she?" I asked, hopeful. He looked at me and for the first time, he sized me up. DAMA is medical speak for Discharge Against Medical Advice. He must have thought I was just a patient relative and now he looked at me like some spoiled brat who just didn't have any form of respect.

"Are you a student here?" he asked.

"Yes, and she is, too. I think she will be scarred if you are not able to get her home especially when she does not want to be here," I continued. "Think about it; you don't want to be here holding onto some crazy person's case when you could be doing something better, bro."

I could barely believe my audacity. He looked as if he was lost in thought for a second and then finally brought out a form to fill.

"You will have to tell Dr. Ajayi, though," he said. "You'll have to sign in her name, too."

I nodded, filled the form, and signed it with her name. I wrote my name down and ended it with *for Dr. Ajayi.* He looked at me again, and looked at Yetunde lying propped on her side, he seemed to pity us, and for good reason. When he left, I quickly packed her things and sent Amaka a message. I told her I would be dropping Yetunde off at her flat around Idi araba because it seemed safer for her than school where she would be the subject of many conversations.

"Are we home yet?" she asked.

"We will soon be on our way," I said. I hoped that would be enough to soothe her.

"Do you love me?" I could not look at her as she asked.

"Let's go, Yetunde." I supported her as we walked out the door, her trolley on one hand and her on the other. I checked my phone again and the message failed to deliver.

Chapter Five

AMAKA

The hospital ward gave me a weird buzzing feeling. Although I had never really been here before now, I felt at home here. Maybe it's because I was studying to be like all these people who tried to take care of Yetunde, who spent all their days and nights here without going back home to their families. Out there, I felt out of place and out of touch with reality but in here, I felt more real.

I was sad, I could feel a dull pit form in my lower belly, but I could not remember what I was sad about. I sat across Yetunde, watching her as she quietly unpacked her bags, she looked so frail, yet when I tried to help her, she refused my help. She took a book and handed it to me, I looked at it very carefully and realized that it was *Ijeawele,* by Chimamanda Ngozi Adichie. I had wanted that book for ages.

"I knew you would like it," she said. Her voice was tired and drained, like the creaking of an old shack at Makoko, the rural community that was close to the third mainland bridge. I held the book in my hands and felt its crispness. Yetunde knew me, she knew how much I love to read books from my favourite author. I just wished she gave me better circumstances, but I didn't know what circumstances would have been deemed better.

"Why won't you let me help you?" I asked.

"I think I am pregnant and it is for Inyene," she said.

What a way to break the news. I wondered if she was really telling me the truth or just making things up. Dr. Ajayi had said that she would have delusions on account of the meds she was taking. I couldn't help but notice that the thought of her being pregnant for Inyene unsettled me a bit, I felt my heart in my throat and I wanted to ask so many questions, but I didn't know where to start.

"I'm getting rid of it, don't worry. I don't think it is something we both want. I don't want an unwanted child," she said this and I felt a wave of sadness cover me followed quickly by relief. I felt so dreadful about how I was not fully understanding of what she was going through, instead, I seemed more focused on the fact that Inyene was now fair game.

She crouched, and I could hear menacing sounds emanating from her, I asked if she was all right, but she didn't say a word. The hospital turned pitch black such that I could not see what was in front of me clearly anymore. I continued to hear ripping noises but I could not move. I opened my mouth to speak but nothing came. Something ripped through her back as she turned to me. Her face was botched and leprous, the room shifted from under my feet and I could feel the vacuum forming as everything lost its form. She lunged at me. I ran as fast as I could. Up ahead, I saw none other than Inyene, but he didn't look like Inyene. He had crystal clear blue eyes and was shrouded in a dark robe. His hands stretched towards me, beckoning. I had an eerie feeling and everything in my bones screamed "Run!", but I couldn't. I was stuck again and this could feel my lifeforce draining and the Inyene-thing feeding on it with glee.

I woke up with a shudder in my room; it was 3:00 a.m. I was drenched in sweat and panting but thankful that it was just a vivid bad dream. My head began to reel with the thoughts of what happened the previous day, Yetunde was in the hospital now with Inyene while I left. I was so tired, but I felt guilty about not staying the night. It would never make sense to me why she would slit her wrists and try to end her own life. I wondered if she had thought about me, or her parents. I couldn't even tell her parents if I had wanted to because she had warned me not to contact them at all so that they wouldn't have to come to Nigeria. *I don't want them to reduce my pocket money,* she had said. I felt it was a stupid thing to do but I had no say in how she handled that relationship. I envied that part of her life as well. Having such a relationship with her parents. I had lost my own parents when I was five years old, so I never knew them. Mama had taken me into her custody then because I was the only child of only children on both my father and mother's side. Mama was my mother's mother and she was more a mother to me than I am sure my mother could have ever been even if she had decided to rise up from her grave. I wondered how Inyene was doing. I had left him alone at the ward last night because he volunteered to stay but today was my turn so I decided to sleep again so that I would be strong enough to take over once it was time.

"What?" I screamed. "What do you mean she is not here, where else would she be?" I could feel the whole ward begin to wake when and I realised that I was shrieking.

"You can't make noise here this girl, people have not woken up yet, go outside and call the person you left her with," the nurse said.

I stepped outside and called Inyene. He didn't pick. He sent a message. "I'm in class, bad timing."

"Yetunde is not at the hospital anymore," I replied.

"She isn't? I left her there this morning when I was leaving for class," he replied.

I tried calling Dr. Ajayi, but her number was not reachable. I called Yetunde again, I must have left thirty missed calls on her phone, but her number was switched off. The prerecorded voice each time droned, "The number you have dialed is currently switched off, please try again later." That couldn't be true. Yetunde's number was anything but ever switched off as long as she was in school. It, being switched off, reminded me of the time we had spent when she came to my house when I was sick. She had complained about how she hated going out of school because electricity was inconsistent and I had agreed. If not to soothe her, at least to help her feel better. But she was right, she did hate when her phone died and I hated it too. Maybe she just decided to disappear like she always did when things got tough, it would not be her first time doing it. Once, when we had a fight, she had switched off her phone and disappeared. I couldn't find her in her room or even in her flat but she reappeared when she felt better and told me that I shouldn't be worried when she went silent, that it meant she needed space and I needed to respect her decision and give her a much-needed time out. Instead of overthinking, I decided to go to school like everyone else until she decided to reach out to me and explain her decision.

Going to class had begun to feel like a chore. Everywhere was abuzz with students moving from one lecture hall to the other. I had not read in weeks, and I had not been active with any of my three study groups. I think I just lacked the right motivation. At this point, I could only cross my fingers and hope to God that I did well in the recently concluded exams because I had been in and out of school so much that I forgot about what being in school was really like. We had all heard about the boy who tried to commit suicide recently because he had repeated multiple times, sometimes it felt like that was all everyone talked about, that was before what happened to Yetunde and now, she was what everyone talked about. Some of my classmates said hello to me, more out of pity than genuine concern and I didn't know if to just accept it or make a quirky reply about how we could all die someday and how Yetunde was the only brave person I knew because at least she tried to take her own life, but that would sound absurd, *the only brave person I knew because she tried to take control of her own life* sounded more appropriate. However, I would still be taken for deliverance by some school fellowship assuming that I had gone mad but I knew that I was speaking a truth that no one really wanted to grapple with. Sometimes those that took their lives were stronger than the rest of us because they didn't just leave their fate to chance.

I tried paying attention in class, but I simply could not, no matter how hard I tried, I never seemed to understand why exactly Yetunde did the things she did: disappearing without a trace, getting pregnant, just doing what she wanted without any thought about the consequences, but yet, I *got* why she did what she did, or I liked to tell myself that I did. I had not yet gotten hold of Inyene, so I tried texting him again in class when the lecturer seized my phone and asked me to come to his office later in the day to pick it up and that was how the lecture ended, with the seizing of my phone and more uncertainty.

When I went outside and saw people gathering in front of the notice board, I remembered that only one thing brought students together in front of some glass cupboard that had boring notices and decrees from the school authorities.

"Results are out!" a classmate shouted. I could hear the "Thank Gods", of the winners and mumbles of those who failed. Crossing my fingers behind my back, I stumbled toward the almighty board and decided that come what may, the least that would happen is that I would pass: I had stopped expecting stellar results like distinctions or credits ages ago.

The crowd seemed to part as I approached the notice board, the looks on their faces reflected more joy than sadness and this made me hopeful that I, too, could have joy at seeing my results. The journey to the notice board felt like a long walk, my feet dragged against the terrazzo pavement and my eyes darted from one group of students to another, all talking about the possible answers to some questions, the reasons why they had not gotten their distinctions and how to prepare better for the next set of examinations. At the notice board, I tracked my matriculation number to my score and beside it, printed in big bold letters:

FAILED. My eyes began to blur as I felt unsteady. My breath quickened and I needed to sit. I sat on the floor and held my head in my hands as the world continued to swirl around me. I didn't need to check Yetunde's number because she most likely passed but I checked anyway and there it was written boldly:

DISTINCTION.

Chapter Six

INYENE

I sat down at my usual spot at Efa and had a feeling of Déjà vu. As I took a long drag of smoke, I saw Yetunde walking towards me again like she did that first night I saw her at Efa. She wore the same dress that flowed like a river of water around her and elevate her as an ethereal being.

"Hey," she said. As I watched her morph back into Amaka. I suddenly felt my cheeks flush and my pulse race.

"Can I sit down beside you?" she asked.

"Sure."

She sat down and brought out her stash. Impressive. She rolled her blunt and placed it in her mouth.

"Can you help?" she asked, gesturing to the blunt.

"Sure," I said. Suddenly aware of how monotonous I sounded. My palms got sweaty again and I had difficulty lighting her smoke for her until she graciously offered to do it herself.

"You don't look so good," she said. I had not looked at myself all day. My shirt was a bit rumpled and I was not sure if I had slept in the past few days.

"I am just stressed," I replied. I had never seen her here before, no matter how much I hoped or prayed to see her, I never did. And here she was, smoking, no less.

"I am just tired. One of those days," she said. It rolled off her tongue like music, she seemed to have no care in the world. I don't know why I felt so unsure of how to react. I wanted to tell her about Yetunde, how I had taken her to her flat and how she had asked me, no, begged me to keep Amaka out of it. I wondered how she would react when I told her I DAMA'd her. I thought she would not take it well and there was no point in telling her things that she would not like to hear but I thought about what I would say if she asked.

"I never knew you smoked, Amaka." I tried to say as matter-of-factly as possible.

"Oh well, we all learn sometime, right?" She relit her blunt and I had a new feeling of closeness with her as if we could talk about things that had happened. She told me about her exams and how she was disappointed in herself for failing. How she had hoped that this time, the outcome would be different and she could find out a better solution for herself. How she felt she had let herself down and I just listened. Not interrupting her, just listening and hoping that my silence would give her more voice.

"Yetunde said you write a lot, wanna write about it?"

"Yeah, I should, I think I should," she said, half-thinking. "You know, I came up with a title: 'Suicide and the Brave Ones Who Do It.' What do you think?"

I liked the sound of it, I just wondered if she really wanted to write about suicide or how her friend almost committed suicide.

"Would you mention me in the article?" I asked.

"Maybe," she said. One of the dealers came up to offer us more weed, he had varying flavours, but Amaka declined.

"I'm good," she said, patting her bag. I wanted to hug her and tell her that it would all be okay. That what was happening was just a phase that would soon be over, but the truth was that I was not sure I would sound convincing enough.

"I think Yetunde just decided to leave when she got better," she said.

"How do you know?" I asked, tense. Aware that I was like a criminal about to be caught red-handed. I had gone back to her flat to check on her, but Yetunde wasn't there. I looked for her every other place I knew, but she was nowhere to be found.

I had gotten a message from her earlier today after which I breathed a well-deserved sigh of relief.

Don't look for me; I'm all right, don't tell Amaka, too.

Looking at Amaka, I wondered if I should tell her or just keep it to myself. I already lied before, so maybe there was no point. Ahmed always said that lying only bred more lies and the truth was never assured as long as I held onto a lie that would potentially ruin it. But I knew that lies were truths that needed to be said.

"What's on your mind?" I asked.

"I'm just remembering that the last time I saw her happy was at my house with you by her side and her telling a story. I wish that we could go back to that," she said.

"Oh, that. There was no light and Yetunde told the most awful cliché story I ever heard," I quipped, surprised at my honesty.

"Wow, coming from someone who clapped his hands off, that's a surprise," she said. She smiled at me and I smiled back.

"I think Yetunde ran away," she said. She began to laugh and slowly transitioned into tears. I felt so uncomfortable, not knowing how to react. She cleaned her tears, took a deep sigh and continued smoking.

The night was warm and still and a new sense of calmness washed over me. We were okay, we were going to be okay. We began chatting about irrelevant stuff. I told her about the one time I and Ahmed got caught by SARS officers and how we were able to escape. She listened, nodded and smiled. She didn't stop me, not once, she listened to me and my mind wandered to how it would feel like to hold her hand. We didn't know when we fell asleep.

I woke up later to find her sleeping on my lap again. Her features were soft. Her low-cut hair was simple and cute. Her pointed nose, high arching chin and pursed pink lips looked inviting. As she slowly began to wake up, I looked away, my heart quickening as she sat up.

"What time is it?" she said. I hadn't bothered to look at my wristwatch, but when I did, I was surprised.

"11:30 pm."

"Wow."

"Yeah."

We started walking down to the hostel in silence. We were close enough to hold hands but did not. It was strange thinking about her more in terms of we than just she. A strange unification that tugged at my heart strings and ached for relief.

"I failed my exam," she said. "But it isn't the end of the world. I just need help with acing it the next time." She looked unbothered when spoke. Like some recording had just rolled off her tongue and she played it as fluidly as she could. I was never failed before, but I knew it wasn't the best experience. I wondered what must be going through her mind. I thought about how to respond to her; holding her hand in silence or simply telling her that she would be okay.

"I could teach you for your re-sit," I blurted. Her expression brightened and her eyes looked grateful. I felt better inside, at least that went well.

"Thank you," she said. I don't know where I gathered the courage, but I took her hand in mine. She was startled for a bit, but she didn't take it away.

Chapter Seven

AMAKA

~~~~~

It was almost 5:00 p.m. and I gathered my books as quickly as possible but I was still late. I had earlier sent Inyene a message that I would be at the classroom by 3:00 p.m., but I had slept off more because of my newfound habit than not getting enough sleep. I felt tired often, so much that I just wanted to fall and die, to rest a final kind of rest that comes with the end of an age.

Inyene's rigour and drilling were out of this world. I called his teaching drilling because it explained why he was a distinction student to me. He knew just how well he had to concentrate on his work and for how long he needed to focus. Deepwork, he called it. Something a white man had concocted that he followed vehemently without question because it worked for him. What surprised me was how he could be so thorough and such a stone head. Ever since we both had our first meeting at Efa, he made it a daily habit to reward all our study efforts with my special package of weed. I refused to tell him the source of course because that would defeat the purpose of my leverage. He seemed to be doing all the work for smoke but at the same time, he was doing it all for me.

The release of our results had ushered in the end of the school year and the school had been mostly empty except for food vendors and a handful of students who didn't go home for holidays. Students who, like me, didn't see the need to go home because they had re-sit examinations or just lived too far to travel home on a whim. I tried to take the shortest route to the cafeteria, but it was sealed off because they had been trying to renovate one of the buildings around there. The building reminded me of the one I had seen around Mushin but it was completed. It gave me a glimpse of what the Mushin building could possibly look like. I took the longer route and decided to call Inyene, certain he would be mad about my lateness. I could hear his voice telling me to do better because re-sits were about a week away.

The clouds gathered outside, turning the sky as dark as a Lagos night. The breeze blew with a bitterness, pushing away most lightweight things in sight including me. I called Inyene but he did not pick up and my phone signal was not as strong anymore. Up ahead, a shrouded and hooded figure in black seemed to be walking towards me. For a moment, I thought it might be Inyene because they were of the same build, except I couldn't see its eyes and Inyene wouldn't dress like that, like some ghoul or goth with a bad sense of taste. I took a turn by the fork on the road to avert it but it followed me still. I began to quicken my pace, walking as quickly as I could down the footpath, but the figure did the same, its pace faster and faster. I felt my heart pounding and the moisture dry from my lips and I began to run as fast as my legs could carry me but before long, I tripped over a stone and fell. I struggled to get my foot out of the gutter, but the silhouette approached me, and I saw its eyes, a crystal-clear blue. I pinched myself; this had to be a dream, I had to wake up now. *Wake up! wake up!* I screamed in my head. But nothing happened. I didn't wake up drenched in sweat and making a Sign of the Cross in the air like I always did; instead, I was knee-deep in a gutter somewhere running away from something that I had once thought only inhabited my dreams. Now my reality was turning into a nightmare. The figure edged closer, walking calmly as if time was no signifi-cant matter. I thought about what to do, who to call and what to tell them when I called. I thought about Yetunde, how she would not be happy that I had met some Grim Reaper of sorts before her. The thought of Yetunde brought tears in my eyes and I began to swoon as the figure came closer and I slipped into unconsciousness.

———

"Amaka, are you okay?" My eyes opened to see Ahmed standing in front of me, worried. I sprung up from the bed, "He was following me!"

Ahmed held me down and called the doctors. When I came to, I noticed how I was attached to intravenous lines and fluids. A nurse was standing beside me counting my respiratory rate and people in other beds looked at me like a lunatic. Parents shielded their children and other adults edged as far away from my bed as they could possibly manage. The sudden recollection of prior events rattled me, the blue eyes and shrouded figure, a man or a beast or a ghost at best, something else at worst. The nurse walked away, and Ahmed looked at me, his eyes showed deep concern about my well-being.

"I came as soon as I saw your WhatsApp message," Ahmed said.

"What message?"

"You were asking about Inyene, then you sent another one that looked like a distress signal. Dr. Ajayi called me because she got a call from the Inspector who he found you lying down on the road, unconscious," he said

"What Inspector?" I asked.

"I'm sorry for startling you, madam." A man dressed in black was seated in the corner of my hospital bay, he sat languidly, hands crossed over his chest.

"I am afraid that I caused all this and I am deeply sorry," he continued. He stood up and walked towards me by the bed.

"I saw you walking down the street and wanted to speak to you, but you took off before I could say anything," he continued.

"I saw something," I said. "It was wearing black, it was chasing me."

The man opened his mouth to speak but stopped himself. I could now fully see his features. He was a short man with a bald head. His potbelly wrestled with his suit as it hung like a kangaroo pouch at the lower part of his belly, asides that, he was fit as a fiddle. Ahmed tensed when he heard his voice as if coming to the awareness that he was in the room as well.

"I am not crazy," I said.

"I am not saying you are crazy, the Inspector found you on the roadside passed out, your leg was in the gutter and now, you are saying you saw something, I don't know if you know how that sounds," he said.

The way he sounded gave me perspective. Of course, I knew how it seemed, how could he think that I didn't know that. The Inspector kept looking at me as if I had a big red label that screamed GUILTY on my forehead. I wondered why a police officer or detective would be following me. I wondered if they were trying to ambush people that took substances and I hoped that I had not been caught.

"Do you take drugs, Ms. Okoro?" he asked.

"No, I don't. I told you that I saw someone or something trying to chase me on the road in my school, I don't feel safe, and what you ask me is if I take drugs?"

"It's a standard question, ma'am, especially given the circumstances in which I found you. I was right behind you, yet you kept running like you just saw a ghost. I wonder why you would run just like that."

At this point it dawned on me how all of this must have looked, how I seemed like a crazy person. But I knew what I saw, it wasn't him; it was a hooded figure with clear blue eyes and I had seen it before in my dreams but never so up close.

"I was dressed in a black raincoat that you can see over there," he gestured at a dark folded material on the chair beside me. "So, I understand why you mistook me for a hooded figure. I was calling your name, ma, so that should have alerted you to the fact that I was indeed a person."

I looked down at my bed, at my bruised leg and hands, trembling. My books were neatly packed together on the cabinet. Ahmed glanced at me, his eyes giving away his inner thoughts. He averted my eyes, but I could see how he looked at me when he thought I was not looking.

"I don't take drugs, sir."

"Weed? Alcohol? Were you under the influence when I saw you this evening?"

"No sir, I was sober and I was on my way to tutorials."

"Okay, ma, but you need to be careful. It was evening when you saw me, it could be possible that your sight was altered. Do you wear glasses?"

"Yes sir, but I don't like to wear them because of the ridge it forms on my nose."

"That explains it," he said as if he had come to the finality of what happened, he had uncovered the truth that made sense to him. Ahmed sighed like a person amused and agitated at the same time. I saw no sign of Inyene when I looked around.

"My name is Inspector Babajide, I am currently in charge of the missing person investigation of Ms. Yetunde Salako," he paused, expecting me to say something but I was still processing the fact that he was investigating Yetunde as a missing person. She wasn't missing, she had just disappeared like she would do from time to time and come back.

"There is something that I need to show you, all of you," he glanced at me and Ahmed. I didn't like how his look made me feel. Yetunde, hearing her name incited a deluge that flowed out of my eyes before I could stop it. I couldn't control myself as I wept and shivered. Ahmed and Inspector Babajide stood awkwardly as they watched me cry. I thought about Yetunde, then I thought about Inyene. It was strange not to find him here with us.

"Inspector, I wish we could meet in better circumstances, but I would like to speak to Ahmed alone if you don't mind."

"No problem, ma, I will be outside." I watched him make his way out of the room.

"Ahmed, where is Inyene?" I asked. Ahmed looked at me, then began to fiddle with his fingers.

"I don't know," he said.

I could tell he was hiding something. I could tell that he didn't want me to know something.

"He was supposed to have tutorials with me and he didn't call even when I was running late, or return any of my calls even now," I stopped myself. Inyene owed me nothing. I couldn't just expect that he would solve all my problems for me.

"Never mind," I said.

Dr. Ajayi was at the entrance talking to the Inspector. She was nodding and laughing like wealthy people do at high society dinners, an attempt at being polite and courteous.

"Did you call her?" I asked Ahmed. He looked to the floor and the ceiling, unsure how to respond but I already knew.

"Why?"

"Can you hear yourself? Ever since Inyene started teaching you, you've been acting strange," he said. "Ever since Yetunde left, you've been acting strange and I think you need to speak to a qualified person."

"You have no right to do that."

"You are right, I don't, but I can't imagine what you must be going through now since Yetunde left and you failed your exams." Hearing that out in the open made it more real now. *Fuck you, Ahmed.* Dr. Ajayi grabbed an empty chair lying around and sat down beside me.

"Hello, dear, how are you today?"

She smiled brilliantly and her pink gums contrasted against her white teeth. I had heard about the Dr. Ajayi effect before but never before had I actually experienced it. Staying around her, I felt calm and welcome like I wanted to tell her all my secrets and hoped that she, too, would be able to divulge something about herself and tell me what to do about my situation. It was like her presence calmed me yet scared me in a somehow non threatening way.

"I think I will be leaving now," Ahmed said, walking away. "Take care of yourself."

"I'm okay," I said, not knowing whether to answer truthfully. Truth was not something I could afford to do properly nowadays and with everything that had been happening, I just wanted to be alone.

"Okay? Well, I guess since you are stuck in bed and got your leg caught in the gutter on your way to your tutorials."

I laughed. The way she said it made it easy.

"I saw something," I said.

"Do you want to talk about it?" she asked.

I did, I wanted to tell her how my heart broke when Yetunde slit her wrists, but how I also felt relief. I wanted to tell her that I was having crazy dreams and I saw Inyene in most of them. I wanted to share with someone before it became too much. Before I lost my mind or whatever remained of it unraveled.

"No."

"Are you sure?"

"Yes, but I could come to your office later. Yetunde always said that your office was great."

She reached out to me and held my hand. I noticed the bracelet she had on wrist. It looked so familiar.

"We are going to get through this, all right?"

"All right," I said. And at that moment, her words felt true.

Chapter Eight

INYENE

I fiddled with my fingers as I sat on the chair in Dr. Ajayi's office. The room was painted pink, and mostly empty asides her table and chair. Dr. Ajayi often said that pink was an uplifting colour, that a pink environment helps patients recover faster. My thoughts moved between the auspicious and the tragic. I tried to focus but I could not. I was tired, tired of feeling stuck and seeing no way out.

"What do you want to talk about?" Dr. Ajayi was seated opposite me, her hands rested on the table.

"I feel bad about this whole thing with Yetunde like it is my fault."

"Why do you say so?"

"I think that if I wasn't there that night, she would be back by now."

"Why do you think so?"

She looked at me and, in that moment, I almost hated her: I hated how she never knew when to stop asking questions. I wished she could just allow me breathe, allow me wallow in this pit where I found myself.

"Do you believe in ghosts?"

"You have to take your drugs, Inyene, no one is going to take them for you," she said.

I laughed, not a genuine laugh; a squeamish one.

"I take them," I said.

She didn't look convinced.

"Have you looked at yourself in the mirror?" she asked.

I shrugged. I tried not to. I knew how I looked, so there was no point in looking. Ahmed had enough of me the day I came back from teaching Amaka carrying a pile of trash. I had jumbled it across the floor and began proclaiming how Iku was coming back. I knew he was. I saw him in a dream and I was certain. I had only wanted to perform the rites when they stopped me. They shipped me off to this place secretly. Dr. Ajayi had been good to me, always welcoming, always forgiving, always giving me a clean slate. At least something that could hold my consciousness together. I felt bad about leaving Amaka the way I did. I saw her calls every day, but I couldn't pick them. What was I supposed to tell her, I'm crazy? I doubted she would be okay with that, besides she had Yetunde to deal with. Yetunde, it had been ages since I last saw her that night after her attempted suicide. It felt like she was dead, and I couldn't help but feel like I killed her, killed her spirit, anyway. Amaka would never forgive me for what I did, letting her go like that. Something more to hate me for.

"You will be going back to school today, that is why I need you to promise me this, if you don't, you will have to come back here. I've already told Ahmed what to do," she said.

She quickly wrote me a prescription, her handwriting hardly legible, but I could make out Chlorpromazine and Haloperidol. I was glad to be going home.

Ahmed greeted me when I returned, and I realised how much I missed having someone sane around.

"You look better," he said. "So much has happened since you left."

"How is Amaka?" I asked. He began to scratch his forehead, a habit of his whenever he was nervous, or worse still, when he was about to lie.

"She is good," he said. I looked at him and knew that I could not believe anything he was saying. But I could not push for the truth either. We walked down the road and he began to update me on certain events. Events even he knew I cared less or nothing about.

"I need to show you something," he said. I was not thrilled to hear what he had to say, I could feel the chill in my bones before he spoke up.

"A lot has changed since you left, the police are involved somehow and I was asked to notify them once you got back," he said. I knew a lot had changed, I could feel it in the air, the whole atmosphere had changed and I could tell that there was no running from this. We walked till we got to the hostel and dropped off my bag, then he led me outside of school to the uncompleted building at Mushin.

Chapter Nine

INSPECTOR BABAJIDE

We were having dinner when my daughter, Demola, mentioned the missing girl from her school.

"Her name is Yetunde," she said. "She's a third-year medical student like me."

"When was this?" I asked. Rita, my wife, interrupted. "We cannot speak about work or missing girls at the table."

People go missing every day, but this was different because it was in Demola's school. My wife and I waited 10 years to have Demola and there hasn't been much luck in that department ever since. She had no special qualities, but she was a lovely girl that I would gladly give my life for. I never showed it, I either gave a grunt or a gruff whenever she spoke, but I wanted the best for her and this new threat in her school was, for lack of a better term, not the best. Yetunde, the classmate, was missing from her school which prided itself as the most secure of all the University Teaching Hospitals. Rita advised me to stay off the case and be home for my daughter, but I knew that I could not. I had to do something.

"You need not involve yourself," she said. She was not happy, but I had to make sure the girl was found; it could have been my own daughter. How could I sleep well when I knew that Demola was not safe?

When I was given the case, I told myself that I would put in my best. The first step would be to locate the victim's best friend, Amaka. I waited around her hostel and watched as she exited the building with a large bag and some books.

She was a major suspect in my investigation and I knew that I had no time to waste. I followed her swiftly. The weather began to change and I noticed how the dark clouds formed and gathered overhead, a harbinger of the coming rain. When she looked back and saw me, she paused for a bit as if unsure of my person, then her eyes widened, she made a run for it. I lunged after her.

"Miss Okoro!" I yelled, hoping that at the sound of my voice, she would stop running. But it was as if my voice acted as a fuel to the fire of her sprint. She ran faster and faster, jumping over logs and debris. I was surprised at her ability to sustain this chase given the state of the threadbare roads filled with many potholes and the occasional shrubs. When she fell, I hoped she would finally give it a rest, but she began struggling to remove her leg from the gutter, looking towards my direction frightened. No, it wasn't fright; it was horror. When I finally got to her, she took one look at me and passed out, yet in her unconscious state, she kept muttering about a certain Inyene who happened to be the victim's love interest.

Now, here I was face to face with him and I was not impressed. The things young people do for love these days. I had gathered the three of them, Ahmed, Amaka, and Inyene to ask them questions. I chose to use Dr. Ajayi's office. It had pink walls and some beautifully carved Nok art effigies with a table set in the middle and two large bookshelves that were colour-coded according to genre and authors. This environment seemed more appropriate than my own office at the station. Ahmed was the first person I interviewed. His fat blob of a face was truly one of the nicest things about him, he seemed harmless. Completely incapable of perpetrating such a heinous act. I brought out a Quran for him to swear on before beginning the interview. I laid it before him and he looked at me, perplexed.

"I'm not Muslim sir, I'm Christian,"

"Then why is your name Ahmed?" I asked.

"It's a long story," he half-smiled.

After replacing the Quran with a Bible, I listened to his side of his story, watching his face and hand movements. He seemed very conscious of his hands. He sat in the chair and he handled all our questions truthfully and with calm, better than most suspects ever did.

"I saw her at a party and she left with Inyene."

"What else happened?" I asked. I was seated opposite him with my pen and paper taking notes, he continued, hesitant.

"We usually hang out at a bar close to school, it's called Efa."

"What do you go to do at Efa?" I asked.

"Just to chill, guy to guy. The whole school goes there," he continued, scratching his forehead. "That was the last time I saw her, they left after."

"It was after this time that Inyene told you they were intimate, correct?"

"Yes."

His phone screen lit up and a familiar face on the screen showed up. It was my daughter, Demola. I was tempted to ask why my daughter was his screen saver, but I decided that it was something that could be handled after the session.

The next person that I interviewed was Amaka. Amaka was more laid back and aloof. She was not as cooperative as I would have wanted, and she sometimes answered my questions with a sigh and coughed in between her answers.

"I told you that I saw something the day you found me."

I did not believe her. At this point, I questioned her mental well-being. Her eyes held a sadness that seemed too much for someone her age to bear. She was frail and seemed to have lost a lot of weight.

"Can you describe what you saw?" She went mute. "Can you tell me about Inyene?" I asked.

She hardly had a response for anything, but whenever I mentioned Inyene, she came alive.

"He would never do something like that, I know Inyene, that is not how he is."

"Why are you investigating us? What have we done wrong? I have a right to understand if I did anything wrong."

"We are trying to know what happened on the day your classmate disappeared."

"It's been weeks and *now* is when you know she is missing? Is the standard not declaring a missing person after seven days?"

"Miss Okoro, we know that you understand your rights here, but your friend's parents are worried because they think she may have been kidnapped. This investigation will help us retrace her steps and hopefully find her in one piece."

Amaka hissed and turned her gaze to the floor, and at that moment a tear fell from her eye, but she was quick to rub it off.

"Are we done here?"

Inyene sat before me. He was very put together even though his health records suggested otherwise. I had collected them from Dr. Ajayi earlier who believed that he would have nothing to do with any of this.

"Do you know anything about Yetunde's disappearance from the hospital?"

I watched him as I asked and noticed that his face is devoid of emotion.

"No, sir."

"I have sufficient evidence contradicting your statement," I replied. "A reliable witness told me that you signed her DAMA form the day she was admitted because she almost committed suicide. My question is why?"

"Who said that?"

"Does it matter? I have the pictures to prove you were there that night."

I flashed him some pictures of himself and Yetunde on the night of her disappearance in front of the hospital ward. He gasped.

"How did you get those?"

"I got them from a reliable source," I replied. I had gotten them from the doctor on duty that night. The young man had reported the incident to his superior as soon as it happened. He found it strange that Yetunde was being led out by a non-relative. He said she took it because he observed that Inyene seemed suspicious and he wanted his conscience clear.

"I felt that I was doing her a favour, I knew her and she was not happy there."

"DAMA means Discharged Against Medical Advice, am I correct?"

"Yes, sir."

"Are you aware of just how much damage you could have caused her even if she were not missing?"

"No sir, doctors can DAMA patients if they don't want to stay."

"Not patients that want to commit suicide, they can't."

I watched as his gaze darkened as I said this. He cracked his knuckles. His patience was wearing thin, he could not hold up his stoic demeanour, he was slipping.

"Does her friend know about this?"

"Amaka?"

"Yes."

"You cannot tell her about this, please. She cannot know, she will never forgive me," he stuttered.

Amaka was sitting in front of me again. More defiant than ever.

"Do you know who released Yetunde the night she went missing?"

"No."

"Are you sure?"

"Yes."

"What if I told you it was Inyene?"

Her face darkened and contorted into a wry smile. She wasn't buying it.

"I know this is some sort of tactic detectives use to interrogate their suspects. It's in the movies." She folded her arms in stubborn resistance. I was not going to get anything out of her.

"What if I bring Inyene to tell you himself?"

I nodded and gestured to my officers to bring Inyene in. They brought him handcuffed, shoulders sagged in surrender. Amaka looked at him and it dawned on her.

"Did you DAMA Yetunde?" she cried.

He nodded in agreement. She looked like she just got hit by a desert storm.

"But I asked you, Inyene! You fucking liar!"

She stood up and walked away. Inyene's head drooped as if heavier than before.

"You are under arrest for your suspected involvement in the case of Miss Yetunde Salako," I looked at Inyene as I said this. He seemed uninterested in what I was saying.

<div align="center">~~~~~~</div>

The uncompleted building was not too far from the school. It was located around the Mushin back gate axis. It was green with algae and reeked of marijuana. The spaces in the compound were boxed in, with little or no room to move. It was a one-storey building without a known owner. One of those buildings the government was planning to demolish. I had asked Ahmed to bring his friends with him so they could see what had been found.

I got a call the day before from an officer who said residents in the area were complaining about a foul smell emanating from the building. The officer and his team had gone in to investigate. And to their shock, they'd found a body without its vital organs. No eyes, heart, kidneys or lungs. The only thing unharvested from the body was the brain and other appendages. Which was curious, because corpses in this state often point to ritual killings, but this appeared to be more like an organ harvest. I requested a DNA test carried out and the result to be cross-referenced with all our missing persons. It was a match. I wanted to see the students' reactions to seeing their friend sprawled lifeless on the floor without innards.

They came in one by one. Ahmed saw the body and looked away, obviously irritated by the grotesqueness of the sight. I asked if he could identify her and the boy went closer. Alarmed, he quickly turned away.

"What is this?" he asked. Perspiration forming on his forehead.

"Can you identify the body?"

"I don't know, is this Yetunde? Are you saying that she was killed?"

He was frantic now, his eyes flaring and wrought with confusion. He tried to grab me reflexively but I moved back, observing his reaction. He broke down in tears not too long after. I asked him to leave and invited Amaka next. She walked in and was shocked upon sighting the body.

"What is this? Is this even legal?"

For the first time, she showed emotion, her face betrayed her fear. She turned around and tried to leave but I asked my officers to hold her back.

"Can you identify the body?" I asked. She looked at me and tears began to flow from her eyes. She looked away. She knew it was Yetunde, her eyes gave her away.

Chapter Ten

INYENE

The floor beneath me rattled as we drove over stones and potholes along the crooked roads. I could hear us stop and refuel, the whizzing sound of the gas pump straining down my ears. We continued and I looked to the officer on my right. He was black, as black as the night's sky. A stench emanated from him. It was a sooty smell, like wet cloth immersed in smoke. He was nodding off, the drool from his mouth hanging loosely, bouncing as the vehicle bounced. His AK-47 rifle was strapped to his shoulders in a sling. We ground to a halt and I heard voices. I decided to take a look, peeping through the raft hanging over the truck and I saw Inspector Babajide conversing with his men. He looked in my direction, but I ducked.

"Take him to the cell," he said.

My heart sank. I was going to be in actual police detention.

The look on Amaka's face when the Inspector led me out of his office is something I would never forget in a haste. Resentment. I doubt she would ever speak to me again. Ahmed was disappointed, too. I could not tell the police that I had DAMA'd her, it was incriminating enough as it was that I had been absent for two weeks, yet here I was and all that was secret and hidden was out in the open. The trunk swung open allowing for light to fill the truck, the man beside me woke up, startled. Nodding and mumbling something that sounded like "Marina."

The sound of the gates opening was strange to me after much silence. The rails creaked as Inspector Babajide came into the room, followed closely by Ahmed. The Inspector looked at me and said something to Ahmed that I could not hear. He eventually left me alone with Ahmed. Ahmed paced for some minutes while avoiding my eyes.

"Would you like to sit down?" I asked. There was a small stool opposite the cell that was for visitors. He looked at the stool, shrugged, then resumed his pacing. Hovering in the corner of the cell was a figure seated on a chair smoking. It was Gozie. I hadn't seen him in a while. They both looked disappointed.

"You should have said something, man," Ahmed finally said. "We told the Inspector that you had nothing to do with anything." He said again, stopping.

I couldn't look at them; I had enough shame already.

"You know I didn't do it," I said.

"I don't," Ahmed said, standing close to Gozie, refusing to meet my eyes.

"How is Amaka?" I asked.

"She will never speak to you again, you should know better," replied Ahmed.

"I could not just leave you here without asking you, not begging you, for the truth."

The air became heavy with his unspoken words.

"Did you kill Yetunde?" he asked.

I could feel my head spin, but I understood why he would think something like that. He looked at me sternly. Gozie looked away, he was waiting for a response as well, a response that I didn't think I had it in me to say anymore. They already felt like I was a killer, I could see it in the way they looked at me.

"I would never do that, and you know it," I said.

"Then why didn't you mention that you DAMA'd her?"

I didn't know why I didn't tell the truth earlier. I remembered how Amaka looked that day when she asked me in the hospital, the day after Yetunde went missing. She had asked me easily, in a way that made it seem easy to also lie about it. She had trusted me; she had come to like me.

"I didn't want Amaka to hate me."

"Good luck, she loves you now."

Ahmed left after dropping off some food and drinks for me. I felt grateful, but it also felt like a waste. Gozie stayed longer.

"We all make mistakes," he said. He was right, but how does one come back from making mistakes over and over again?

"I wish I had said something," I said.

"Me, too," he replied.

We both sat there, staring at the ceiling as time slipped by. The officers came into the room later and confiscated all the foodstuff that Ahmed brought for me.

"We will give it to you small, small," an officer said. I recognized him from the truck. He was the black officer. I noticed that his eyes were bloodshot, no surprise there. They had a new gleam now, one of greed. I knew I would not get anything back. I curled up closer to my bed while Gozie sat in the stool beside the rails. When night came, I had never felt so alone.

～～～～～

Dr. Ajayi came to visit me on a sunny Sunday morning. I knew this because the prisoners usually had an early morning prayer session with some pastor from a Pentecostal denomination.

She was dressed casually; I was used to seeing her in her ward coat or wearing some formal dress but today, she was in Ankara pants with a plain top. She even wore a hat and a black bracelet that seemed eerily familiar. We joked about how she was my spec if she were not so old. She smiled at me, maintaining the empathic outlook that she usually had. Then her look turned serious.

"Why didn't you tell me that you let Yetunde go home?"

I looked away. I knew that she had hoped that I would be truthful about it, but I couldn't tell her that it was because of Amaka.

"I forgot to."

"You can't forget something like that," she replied. "What is going on, Inyene?"

"I was ashamed, I thought Amaka would hate me if she knew. I didn't think she was going to get killed."

I could feel the air get stuck in my throat as tears welled up in my eyes. She put her hand through the bar and placed it on mine. I wanted to pull away, but she resisted and clasped it tightly. I cried, I let it all out, all the suppressed feelings that I had for the past few weeks, I let it out.

"She said she was pregnant and all I could do was tell her off, what kind of person am I?"

Dr. Ajayi slowly massaged my hand and waited patiently for my tears to flow.

"You are a human being who makes mistakes," she said. "Don't beat yourself up for what has already happened."

"But everyone thinks I killed her! I didn't. After leaving school I came straight to you, even you can corroborate that."

"And I will. You have to exercise patience. You know the way this country is. I will talk to the Inspector, but you need to calm down and take care of yourself."

She brought out a container filled with medications from her bag and handed them to me across the bar.

"I've done a refill for you myself as usual," she said. "You won't stay here for long, I promise." She left in the early hours of the afternoon. Her words filled me with hope.

Chapter Eleven

AMAKA

Everything tasted of blood. Mama had offered me her best *Ofe nsala* and pounded yam, but it tasted like blood. The metal tang of iron, the grazing against my teeth. It was Yetunde's blood, of this, I was certain.

Ozioma decided to follow me out as a way to avoid Mama's nagging. I read that walks help you think things through and having Ozioma around was a welcome idea. At least I was not alone with my thoughts. We went to Mushin market again to buy the ingredients for our Jollof rice for this Sunday. I was very ready to do something other than think about the past few days. She showed me a vendor who sold some red tomatoes; they appeared red enough to give Jollof its characteristic orange hue. The peppers were yellow, however, and the seller seemed uninterested in bargaining for the price we wanted.

After purchasing our goods, I told Ozioma to go home without me, I needed to be alone now, I had so much to process. Inyene was in prison for killing Yetunde. Not actually killing her, but withholding information. Yet I remember that when I had asked him about Yetunde, he said nothing. However, I noticed that when he lied, his brows scrunched together like folded cloth. He lied to me and I noticed but decided to let it go. I thought he would say it when we spoke at Efa, but he didn't. It made no sense to me why he would do that. I felt so dumb in front of Inspector Babajide. He was trying to wring out a statement from me, something incriminating, but I was just as clueless as everyone else. Since I saw Yetunde's body I knew I could never remain the same. I first felt a pang, like a blow to the stomach. Her body was in that uncompleted building we had passed several times on our way out of school. Seeing her body did something to me. She had no eyes, and no breasts, the Inspector also said that she had no private parts or vital organs. The only thing that I could identify her with was that bracelet she liked to wear around her wrist. The Inspector had said that the body was confirmed to be hers but I don't believe it. I was scared and broken, I was in denial.

Walking down the road, I suddenly found myself in front of her hostel. I hardly remembered how I got here, all I recall was my walking and walking. Maybe there was something here that could help, something that could show me what exactly happened to her. Her room was intact, everything was in place. Her bed was covered in dust and sprawled across it was a huge bag filled with clothes. I had not been here since she went missing. I had come from time to time to check on her, but as days became weeks, I stopped, accepting that she would contact me when she was ready.

The floor was dusty, too, and littered with her shoes. A curtain hung from the window, tattered and tired against the wind. Her ceiling fan was rusted; I tried turning it on, but it made such a noise that I left it as it was. I saw her laptop on the reading table beside the window. I opened it and I typed in the password: INYENE. Typical. I knew that had to be her password because it was once my name. Yetunde's passwords were her favourite people in the world at the moment. I saw her videos on twerking and makeup. I saw some pictures of us, of herself and Inyene. She looked so happy and full of life. I didn't realise when my cheeks became wet with tears.

I was just about to close the laptop when I saw an emblem attached to a folder. It was shaped like a bracelet, like the bracelet she always wore. It was black with smooth rounded edges.

I opened it and saw a list of videos. Numbered one through five. I clicked on video one.

She was laughing in the video. She was dressed in a yellow top and had her natural hair tied up in two big pigtails.

"Hi, guys! So…I have started going to therapy today and my therapist gave me the cool bracelet, can you see?"

She moved closer to the screen and put the bracelet close to the camera.

"She said that it will make all my wishes come true."

The video ended and I clicked the next one, eager. This time, she was dressed in a black dress and her hair was still up in pigtails. She seemed stressed with bags underneath her eyes. She looked happy but lacked her usual radiance.

"Hi, again guys! So, my dream did come true! Inyene is officially mineeeee! I knew this was going to happen and I am so happy!"

I clicked on the third video and I was shocked. She looked disheveled, her hair was a mess, her eyes twitching and she was trembling. She had a red dress on and her hands seem to be stained with a red substance.

"Guys, I am officially in trouble, be careful what you wish for because you will surely get it. I don't know who to talk to or what to say, I wish I could talk to Amaka right now, she would know what to do."

I clicked on the next video and when it came on, she was not seated there anymore. The chair was empty, and I search around the video to see if there is any sign of her. Then suddenly, a figure —dark, menacing, a half-man, half-beast with blue eyes—appeared in the place of hert, head bowed, hands folded. It began to say something. The room became darker then I heard its cold raspy voice. A voice that sucked the life out of the room.

Amaka.

I jolted up and dropped the laptop, my chest pounding. The screen went off. I looked around at the room to be sure there was no one there. Then I carried the laptop and put it in my backpack and ran away from the room as fast as possible.

I returned home late and Mama was worried.

"Are you feeling better?" she asked. Of course, I wasn't feeling better. My friend had just died. I didn't know what it was that I saw on her laptop, Inyene was in prison and I just felt so lifeless inside.

"You feel different," she said. "There is a presence around you that feels different, and I think we should pray." I didn't have the mental or physical energy to argue, so I just did what she asked. We said a short prayer then I went to my room and shut the door, hopeful that Ozioma would not come knocking unexpectedly.

I heard footsteps and sat up when I saw a shadowy figure seated across from me in the room. The room was dark and I could hear sounds of beating drums and ringing *shekeres*. The shadowy figure stepped before me and I could feel my impending doom.

It stepped into the light and I could see that it was Inyene, the way he looked at me sent chills up my spine. His eyes were crystal blue and his crooked hands were pointed at me.

"You are next," he said. I could feel all the joy leave my body as his hands came and wrapped itself around my neck.

I woke up with a jolt, holding my arm around my neck. I could feel the chill in the room. The fan was still rotating lazily, but there was light now. The door was wide open and what looked like a mist disappeared from the front of my eyes. I screamed. Mama came in instantly and asked what was wrong. I kept pointing outside and I felt the chill leave my bones. I slumped on her body and cried.

"I think we need to take you to my Pastor," she said.

The Bread of Life Christian ministries was a church headed by Prophet Isaiah. Mama said that he came to Nigeria to preach the message of salvation just like Isaiah in the bible

He was an Isaiah incarnate. Bullshit. The candle-lit building was white on the exterior. The interior had Victorian styled church windows. Its altar was made up of marble and ceramics. Prophet Isaiah was standing at the podium dressed in trousers and a shirt. He was young for someone who claimed to be a prophet, maybe in his early thirties. He shook Mama's hand when we came in. Mama reciprocated and kissed his hand. He looked at me and smiled.

"The Devil wants to take this one, but God is going to overcome," he said while placing his hands on me, and beginning to praying in tongues. I was too tired to stop him and watched instead. Mama joined him in prayers raising her voice to the heavens. I could feel my head burn as his palm touched my forehead and it felt like whatever he was doing was working. He stopped suddenly and looked at me, the lights of his eyes dimmed.

"Why didn't you bring her since?" he asked. Mama looked at him and shrugged.

"We thought she was not feeling too well, but with everything that has been happening to her, we began to see that it was beyond the physical."

He nodded and continued praying in tongues, then brought out a bottle of olive oil. He asked me to come closer and then poured the whole bottle on my head. He breathed into my face, and I cringed, his mouth odour, pungent.

"You festering spirit, I bid you come out of her now!" he commanded.

Nothing happened. I only felt a tinge of exhaustion as he said this. He held my hand and looked intently into my eyes.

"Everything is going to be fine; God has delivered you," he said. I could not open my eyes for fear that the oil would flow into them, but if I squinted hard enough, I could see the outline of his face as he said this to me.

He then called Mama aside and they discussed in hushed tones. They occasionally glanced at me and Mama made some very shocked and funny expressions. They disbanded and he came straight to me.

"Me and your Grandma are going to your school, but I will stay at home," he said and I was too tired to disagree.

Chapter Twelve

INYENE

~~~

I was in the cell room for four days. I used a metal pointer to carve the numbers on the wall just like in the movies, and with each carving, I wondered what was going on outside these walls. I would either stay here forever or find a way to prove my innocence. I wished I had told Amaka what I did, but that would do nothing now. I paced around the cell room and processed my thinking as much as I could. I hardly saw Inspector Babajide these days. Gozie came from time to time and we talked a lot, but he hardly stayed too long. He seemed always busy with one thing or the other. Dr. Ajayi gave me a handball to play with for stress relief.

"You can just bounce it off the wall when you seem tired or confused," she said. Bouncing it off the ceiling and catching it became my favourite thing to do. And in one of those moments, I saw a figure at the corner sitting.

"Gozie, just go already, I have drugs now and I don't think that I am still supposed to be seeing you," I said, not giving him a second glance. The figure remained silent. I looked closer and I realised it was not Gozie. I could feel my heart begin to pound.

"Who's that?!" I yelled. The shadow came closer and closer until I saw it in the light, it was me. I quickly touched myself to be sure that I was seeing clearly.

"I am going to get her," it said. "She belongs to me!" I noticed that the room began to feel cold like all the joy had been sapped out of it. It was as if this was real but surreal. I couldn't
~~~

tell the difference anymore. The thin line was slipping. It had been so long since I took my drugs, I'd been too upset to do so. Dr. Ajayi was right because if there was any shred of doubt that I was going bonkers, this cleared it.

Chimera.

That is what she called it when I had my first episode. That was the first time I heard the word. She said it meant something that existed in the imagination, but was impossible in reality. She said it was what has started happening to me again, she had refused to call me what I was, crazy. This being in the room stared at me for a couple of minutes before speaking. It was inaudible. I felt transfixed as it moved slowly towards me. I felt my body weaken and my insides churn. I pinched myself because I knew it had to be a dream, but I felt stuck. I felt paralysed. I tried to call one of the officers, but I could barely hear myself speak. I was just about to close my eyes and surrender when I heard a voice calling me. I felt shaken and I opened my eyes to see the Inspector with Amaka's grandmother and a young man at the entrance of my cell. Once inside my cell, the young man began to set candles on the floor and Amaka's grandmother assisted him. They made a semicircle and he hovered over me; his face contorted in prayer. I looked around, but Amaka was nowhere in sight. Inspector Babajide stayed at a corner, watching the whole thing.

The Inspector had come to my cell earlier, reeking of cigarettes and alcohol. He sat opposite me in a chair, arms folded across his chest as if about to question me again.

"Amaka's grandmother is coming with a Pastor today," he said. "She believes that all she has been going through is due to a supernatural occurrence."

"What does that have to do with me?" I asked.

"The Pastor said he heard your name in a vision after praying for Amaka and decided to perform a deliverance on you." I was stunned when he said this and the Inspector didn't come off as someone who believed in the fictitious.

"But sir, is this allowed?"

From his seat, he bluntly said: "Prayer is allowed."

"Also, you don't have a good history of having the right kind of thinking,"

"How do you mean?"

"I spoke to your psychiatrist, and she said she has been trying to get you to take your meds, but you have refused, that is the major reason you are here. You need to be monitored."

Now here this *man of God* was about to perform some weird ritual on me with Amaka's grandmother and Amaka was nowhere in sight. Signs that I needed to rethink my life choices more. I should have just taken my drugs. He poured oil on my forehead and began to speak in tongues like they do in new generation Pentecostal churches. The ones Amaka said she hated attending, her grandmother's church. I slowly felt myself slipping, like I had no control of my body, as he prayed, I heard myself fall. I was woken up by the Pastor who smiled at me and congratulated me for celebrating my victory over the enemy. I was confused about what was going on when he said that he had fasted and prayed and cast out some demon from me.

"You were far gone my son, but God is faithful," he said.

I looked around the cell to realise we were the only ones there. Amaka's grandmother left without saying a word to me. Inspector Babajide came into the cell. His mood was dour. He sounded disappointed and furious.

"There is no point holding you here anymore. Your guardian has demanded your release based on a lack of evidence." I sighed, relieved. I was happy to be leaving. He led me out of the cell and I reclaimed all my belongings from the reception. I trudged to the front door. I could feel the Inspector's eyes boring into my back. I could see the face of a new detainee, a young man not much older than myself, there was blood streaming down his face and he was held up by one of the officers. I saw him and I felt an overwhelming sadness. I was lucky.

Chapter Thirteen

AMAKA

I had observed how Mama looked at me, like I was some fragile thing that could break at the slightest provocation. She watched me like a hawk and hardly left me by myself. I called Inyene when I heard he was released from detention. I was happy he could come back now, and at least I could forgive him now that I knew he was not a killer. He sounded normal over the phone like police detention had not changed him yet he sounded different. He seemed to choose his words more carefully. We planned to see each other later because he still owed me tutorials. I asked Mama for her car keys for the first time in a while. I could not remember the last time I drove. She smiled at me, she even asked me to take as much time as I needed. The sudden change was strange but I figured she was tired of all the drama anyway.

"Help me go to the market and buy foodstuff for this weekend. I am making *nsala* and pounded yam." I nodded and decided to go alone. Ozioma was not around anyways and I needed to clear my head again. So much had happened, but much was going back to normal as well.

The market seemed more empty than normal and I had to ask why. The Hausa seller, a mallam, selling me carrots was part of a community of other mallams selling similar goods. His wheelbarrow was filled with carrots, cabbages, cucumbers and lettuce, just what I needed. I could tell something was wrong with how he sighed before he began to speak.

"Na that hospital dey cause problem. Since that girl die, *na so we dey* find dead body of plenty animals." That sounded very strange because I had heard it differently. But of course, people will relate normal occurrences with the supernatural, other reasons may not just seem as believable.

I packed my goods and made my way to the back gate of school when the stench hit me. The school smelled like rotting flesh. I could see men gathering animals from the gutter and other parts of the sewer. I saw Inyene up ahead, and he flagged me down. It felt awkward opening the door and letting him into the car. He looked good, better than I expected. He looked out the window as I began to drive, none of us saying anything to the other. I broke the silence.

"So, it's been a while huh?" I croaked.

"Yeah."

I tried to keep my eyes on the road. I had a million things to say but didn't know how best to start. He didn't look directly at me either, I could tell from my side view that he was focused on the road. I continued, "How have you been?"

"I have been okay. Pushing, you know." He fiddled with his keys as I continued to drive down. I saw some dead rats on the road and some cats as well.

"What is happening in this school?" he asked. I nearly had the same question, but I had an idea of what was going on.

"I heard someone poisoned the sewage system or so, a new type of extermination, the pests were getting too much."

"That makes sense, they were getting too much," he said. We both laughed as heartily as our voices could allow without making it seem like we didn't care.

"What have you been up to?" I asked. "Except getting out of detention."

He laughed and said, "I should ask you the same question."

"I have something I need to tell you," he said. I could feel the blood draw from my cheeks, maybe he finally wanted to confess about killing Yetunde and then tell me so that I could help cover up for him. "I have schizophrenia," he mumbled. It didn't make sense before, but thinking about it now, it all made sense. The disappearances, his strange way of dressing.

"Wow, so you are crazy now?"

"Sort of; I take my drugs, but when I don't, I tend to slip. I see someone, his name is Gozie, he isn't real, but he is sort of an alter ego. He is a pain in the ass."

Now I was scared, I wondered if he was going to tell me about how he went about killing people. I squeezed to the steering wheel.

"Is that all you want to tell me?" I asked.

"I am also sorry for not telling you I DAMA'd Yetunde," he said.

"It's fine," I replied. "So, your schizophrenia, is that why you like to disappear?"

"Yeah." We both chuckled.

"I also think that I am in love with you," he said. "I know it sounds weird, but all that has happened over the past couple of weeks have given me time to think. I think we could try being together and see how it goes. I get it if you turn me down." I thought about it when I looked at him and smiled to myself. I kept driving, actively avoiding his eyes.

I dropped him off at his hostel and drove straight home. I could still feel his eyes on me as I drove away. This was already too much for one day. It's all so crazy how the world had changed so much since Yetunde died. Now, her boyfriend said that he loved me. Getting home was a struggle because of this stupid Lagos traffic. I met Mama down the stairs as she welcomed me with a plate of nsala and pounded yam. She looked at my hair, now unkempt and growing longer.

"When you finish eating, I will comb it for you."

I sat down and quickly began to devour the food, I rolled each fluff of pounded yam into a ball that I thought I could swallow, but ended up choking on some. When I was done, I washed my hands and sat down at Mama's feet. She rubbed her hands through my hair, unknotting the curls and gently loosening the tied-up ends.

"When will you cut your hair?" she asked.

"I want to grow it," I replied. I didn't turn around, but I could sense her smile.

"How are you feeling?" she asked. I began to smile to myself.

"Happy," I said. For the first time, I was.

I found myself at the uncompleted building again. The fact that Inyene told me he loved me filled me with dread and hope at the same time. What he said about Gozie, also made me feel safe, like I could tell him anything. I could tell him my dreams and visions and about what I saw on Yetunde's laptop but I also knew that he had been in prison and I didn't want to risk him going away again. I carried only a flask and fanny pack with me so that I could travel light. Ozioma had told me exactly what I needed to do. We had an extensive chat after I told her all I had found on the laptop.

"I knew, that is why I knew the deliverance mama did would not be enough," she said. We went through all the documents and found several guides that showed me what needed to be done.

"You just need to count from one to ten, it will all be over soon," she said. She already told me the steps and I just needed to act it out. I was scared. I looked around to be certain no one was following me, I triple checked before I came into the compound so that I would not need to feel like I was being watched.

"But you will be watched," she said. It can sense your presence when you come close enough to the site. It will smell your fear or will, it gives him power, all the power he needs."

I already had all the odds stacked against me. Each rustle in the weed-infested compound sent shivers down my spine. I waited till the moon was full at midnight.

"That is when you can make penance," she said. Ozioma's knowledge of the subject matter bothered me, but I was glad I had her for this. She had been adopted from our village when she was younger, her father was the village priest and she had learned a thing or two. Mama always complained that she never prayed and that she still worshipped traditional gods. Ozioma never took it personally. She was a normal child and she didn't wear red cloth or tie palm leaves on her head the way they do in movies. She went to church with us as an obligation, but she always prayed to her family god. She found out about the laptop when I came back from my walk. I was searching Yetunde's laptop and found a document tagged "Why." It was a scanned handwritten document: Yetunde's suicide note.

Dear someone,

If you are reading this, then I am gone.
I delved deep into the dark magic in my room at night and began to feed off from Amaka's energy first. She seemed the most likely source of energy. She had an unstable mind and that was a major ingredient. I went to that building at Mushin every two weeks and saw him appear to me as if from smoke, his form taking the shape of what I wanted the most, Inyene. I've always wanted Inyene and Amaka took him away from me. The painful thing is that she does not know. I see the way he looks at her and he will never look at me this way. Not while she lives. After everything, I have done for her. She has decided to betray me and I choose to return the favour. I summoned Iku and he said he would help me, but he only needed to possess her body. I followed his orders. I collected her undies, I added drugs to her meals, and I

gave her my special weed. I did everything he asked me to do. I only wanted Inyene to want me and not her.

Then it all went wrong when Inyene said he didn't want me. I asked Iku to change his mind, but he said he could not control love. That was when I knew that he could not be trusted. I stopped trying to communicate with him and told myself that it would all be okay. But he kept showing up in my dreams or on the road. He kept following me around and tracing my every footstep. I told no one about this.

Iku had not had enough of me yet, so he tried to possess me. I fought very hard to be free of him, but he would not let me go. He told me that I was his bride and he was my Inyene.

I blackout from time to time to find my room arranged differently or worse, some animal dead in a corner with blood stains on my palm. The more he came, the more he claimed that I was not allowed to be human anymore. As time progressed, I could feel his hand as he touched me and told me that I was not allowed to be human anymore. I gulped, but I knew he was right and I had to make this right. I decided to kill myself so that he would not get me first. If you are reading this, I hope he didn't. This all feels like Chimera, like it's not real, but feels so real at the same time.

At the end of the document was a picture of the bracelet she always wore. I remember sitting still and looking at a corner in my room, expecting Iku to come again but nothing happened. I pored over the files but the bracelet kept standing out in all her videos. It was black with two blind-ending studs that formed a semi-ring. I was rewatching another video footage when Ozioma walked in and screamed that I turn the laptop off.

"You do not know the evil with which you are trifling with," she had said and claimed to have the solution for ridding myself of such evil. Her solution was so absurd initially that I didn't want to do it. She had given me a flask of blood and I didn't know how exactly she got it. I pleaded with her to do it for me, but she said that I had to take my own life in my hands.

———

I checked my wristwatch and it was midnight. I took a deep breath and got to work. Carrying the flask of blood in my hand, I walked into the building and Iku was standing before me as if expecting me just as Ozioma had predicted. Ozioma gave me her little cauldron and told me exactly what I needed to do.

"Put it on fire and coax him. Then tell him that you beg for mercy," she said. Seeing Iku now, I didn't know if I should scream or keep working but Ozioma had said that if he had wanted to harm me, he would have already, so I just had to do what needed to be done. I only hoped it would work. I walked lightly, one foot following each heel as Iku's gaze never left me. He stood in a dark corner, his form was humanoid but three times the size of the average man. He was bald with broad shoulders with everything else hidden beneath a black cloak of panther-like fur.

I continued this way until I was finally at the spot where Yetunde was found and quickly went to work. I poured the blood from the flask into the small cauldron. I laced some blood on my forehead when I heard a sound, a whistling in the trees. Not sure of what to expect, I looked back to see that Iku had vanished and in his place was Inspector Babajide, along-side Inyene.

Chapter Fourteen

INYENE

~~~~

I had told Amaka the truth and it finally weighed off my chest. She didn't react as I had feared, she just listened. After dropping me off, I called Ahmed to pick me up so we could hang out. He drove in with Demola, whom I was meeting officially for the first time. I had met her unofficially at Efa. She had dark hair and wore loud makeup, she seemed very chatty, too. She was not my type. I had to sit behind and listen to her speak about how school was now a graveyard since this whole Yetunde incident. Ahmed nodded pleasantly as he listened to her. He was very into her. I smiled quietly.

We dropped her off at her hostel and she said goodbye to us. She bought us drinks and gave Ahmed a kiss which made him blush. I pictured Amaka doing something like that for me, telling me goodbye and kissing my cheek, the thought of it excited me.

"Do you love her?" I asked as I joined him in the front seat, making certain Demola was out of earshot. He paused and looked at me then looked forward and started the engine.

"I do." He didn't look at me when he said this, but he didn't fiddle with his hands or touch his brows or play about it, he seemed serious about her and his love for her.

"How do you know?" I asked, unsure how to relay the fact that I just spilled my guts to some girl whose friend I had also dated.

"You just do, man," he said as he started the engine.

"I think I love—"
~~~~

"Amaka?" he asked, clearly amused. I was surprised and looked away to prevent myself from blushing.

"How did you know?" I asked.

"You call her name in your sleep, you trail her everywhere, you practically hallucinate about her!"

There was an awkward pause and for a minute I pretended to have no idea what he was talking about.

"I'm kidding. It's just obvious, the way you act around her."

"I told her."

"What did she say?"

"Nothing."

"Did you expect more?"

I did expect more, with all the craziness in the world right now, I expected more. I wanted her to know everything about me. I told her everything.

"I told her about Gozie."

"You what?"

"I told her, that is why she probably didn't say anything."

He looked at me and began to laugh. His laughter was so loud and contagious that it almost pissed me off.

"You will be fine," he said.

As we reached the front of our hostels, a police van came into view with Inspector Babajide pacing in front of it. Once he saw us, he signaled that we should follow him. We silently left Ahmed's car and went into the truck. We drove down the now familiar path to the police station.

At the station, we were let into Inspector Babajide's office by some of his men and heard him screaming orders at his deputies. He barged in, face filled with perspiration, eyes blazing. Something was up and I silently prayed that it had nothing to do with me.

"Where is Amaka?" he asked. I was puzzled. Amaka had dropped me off some hours ago and had gone straight home, that much I knew.

"I just got a call from Ozioma, Amaka's half-sister, her grandmother is dead. In the same way that Yetunde was found. Missing vital organs," he said, not bothering to sit down, just pacing anxiously. I had never seen him so riled up.

There was a sinking feeling in my stomach, I thought that all this was over now. Sigh. He began rounding up his men and asked myself and Ahmed to follow them. They had tagged Amaka, a prime suspect on the run.

"Amaka would never do this," I said. Inspector Babjide looked at me frantically.

"Even if she didn't do it, what would you have me do? People are dying. I have to do something."

I searched his face and I understood where he was coming from. I hoped that Amaka had nothing to do with any of this.

We went back to the uncompleted building first. I could feel the emptiness of the space. I took my pills just to be sure that I was stable. Inspector Babajide came to stand beside me, he looked worn and tired.

"I thought it was you, you know, you had a motive, and you were crazy," he said. "I asked her grandma why she had a pastor pray for you at the prison, but she said the deliverance was not for you, it was for her granddaughter."

I took in all he said. I felt stigmatized because of how he branded me.

"She went on to explain some weird folktale that involved a God of Death or something, a story that still makes no sense to me," he continued. He went off and kept barking orders at his men. I could see Ahmed in a corner on the phone, probably speaking to Demola.

I began to ponder on all that he said and I went back to the day when myself and Yetunde visited Amaka. Her sheer curiosity about the subject matter astounded me, but I tried not to get too bogged down by the details. I didn't trust the Inspector. He messed up the first time and I was certain that he is just as wrong now.

I was shocked to see her standing there with blood on her face and a pot of fresh blood. It was incriminating enough that she was a suspect but being caught in the act was a whole different ball game. Inspector Babajide and his team quickly handcuffed her. One of the deputies mistakenly tipped the bowl over and the blood spilt on the floor.

"Let me go! I need to finish this! This is important, please!" she screeched. I could not believe what I was hearing.

"Can I speak to her?" I asked. The Inspector shook his head.

"We need to take her in for questioning, Inyene," he said.

As they cuffed her and moved her to the vehicle, I had so many questions that I wanted to ask. Why would she do something so cruel to her grandmother but I knew I wouldn't ask because she would never tell the truth. She had so many opportunities to, but she chose not to.

"You have to believe me," she said as they brought her towards me. She quickly handed me a folded paper. I quickly hid to read it as the police officers dragged her off and I stood there transfixed. I had an idea.

〜〜〜〜〜

Ahmed offered to drive me to visit Dr. Ajayi. We were parked in front of her house now; I carefully contemplated what I was going to say, what needed to be said.

"Demola is calling me, she is probably worried, will you be okay," he asked. I nodded.

Dr. Ajayi's house was at one of the farthest corners in school. It was lined between four other buildings of similar structure: quaint uniform burgundy and cream coloured three-storey buildings. I sucked all the courage and walked towards the farthest one. I held my phone in my hands and searched for the record button, I clicked it and quickly placed it in my pocket. I was about to ring the bell when the door opened and Dr. Ajayi, standing at the doorway, smiled at me. She welcomed me inside.

"Would you like something to eat?" she said. "I just made rice and stew." I declined. I held the paper in my hands, curled and tight in my grasp. Her house was warm and very organized. The living room had a retro look with ancient history paraphernalia, the books were stacked up on shelves and colour-coded, red for horror, white for biographies, green for Nigerian History. Her couch felt very cold as I sat on it, there was no room for dust and cobwebs. She came out again with a bottle of Coke and a plastic cup, then she set it before me. I took note of the arm bracelet she had on, pretty sure of what it was now, even though it once eluded me.

"I like your bracelet," I said. Truly admiring it like a piece of art. "You have great taste."

"Thank you, dear," she said. Her smile strained.

"I notice that you like religious artefacts, don't you?" I asked.

"Yes, they are a real thing of beauty to have around."

"I am learning that you were the one that taught me to appreciate beauty," I said. She chuckled nervously and poured herself a cup of coke.

"So, what brings you here today? I don't do sessions in my house, but I could make an exception just for you."

"Thank you, ma," I replied calmly. She turned on the television. I shook my head.

"I'm a good, ma," I said. She took note and quickly sat down on the couch across from me.

"You were Yetunde's doctor, right?"

"I like to keep my client information confidential." She replied.

"You know, I wondered where I had seen the bracelet she liked wearing before and it looks like you both have the same thing.

"I am sure we do, it is a very common bracelet."

"I was thinking, or rather, I have been thinking recently about everything that has been going on," I continued. I was strangely calm for everything that was on my mind.

"You have? We all have my dear, we all have really," she replied composed as ever.

"Then I remembered something. You had Yetunde's private information and mine, too."

"I should think so?"

"When the Inspector questioned us, he didn't even hesitate to arrest me because he had evidence beyond a reasonable doubt." She remained silent now, pensive, watching where this was headed.

"Then, there was the issue of my drugs. Even when I took my drugs, I still saw Gozie speaking to me. He is here, by the way." She stood up from her seat now with her drink in hand, clearly worried.

"Are you sure you don't need to go to the hospital, dear?"

"Then Amaka gives me Yetunde's letter and it is addressed to someone, but I know her writing, this is not her handwriting. She wrote on the gifts she gave me and she liked to serenade me with videos and one or two poems, so I am pretty sure I remember her handwriting, but Amaka does not remember because she is under some kind of spell."

Dr. Ajayi's warm smile turned dour as she took in my words. The room fell silent.

"So, I put two and two together. I saw Chimera in the letter and I know you are the only person who uses that word and Yetunde was not verbose enough to keep that kind of word in her head. I figured out that maybe there is some kind of spell, or maybe I am mad or not mad, but I am certain that you are causing all this."

I quickly brought out the folded paper Amaka gave me. At the bottom of the printed letter was the drawing of the bracelet that both she and Dr. Ajayi wore. She dropped the plastic cup and walked across the room to meet me. She came uncomfortably close to my face.

"Are you sure you are okay?"

"I am."

"Because you don't have any proof to back up your baseless arguments."

Her tone had suddenly changed. It was no longer high-pitched and welcoming, it was stoic, almost bland. Her demeanour also changed, her smile shrinking into a scowl.

"What do you mean?"

She began to laugh, maniacally now, then her voice slowly transitioned to a hissing sound.

"It is your word against mine."

"I just want to know why you do it. What do you gain from playing around with the lives of some young gullible people that look to you for guidance?"

She stood up. She went to her cabinet and brought out a syringe. She brought out a bottle of fluid and drew out the fluid into the syringe.

"You want to know why?" she asked. "Are you sure?"

I secretly didn't want to know why. I wanted to take it all back, I wanted to be wrong. I wanted her to snap me out of this dream that I can't seem to wake up from.

The room began to darken, the windows slammed open and close and the floors began to vibrate. I felt the presence that I had become familiar with as I saw Dr. Ajayi's shadow lengthened into a chimera. It was terrifying to watch her become distorted as her shadow tripled in size and intertwined with her physical body, spreading over her skin like a disease.

"Should there be a reason for doing anything at all?" she said, her voice deepening as she spoke while walking toward me with the syringe. "I have always wanted children, you know. I prayed to God for years and look how that has turned out. Then I said I would take care of all my patients like my own children."

She sat down beside me and straightened out my shirt. I don't know why I suddenly could not move. I could only look at her face, my body was transfixed. Her eyes had turned an unnatural blue, she had fangs that jutted out from her teeth and her shadow towered above her from behind.

"But as you can tell, that didn't happen. I went to some village in Ogun where I was told that if I prayed to Oya, she would give me children. I prayed and prayed and prayed and fasted. Like I have never before. She never answered me."

I nodded, trying to follow.

"When I saw that she was not forthcoming, I called on the other side of things, I called on her rival, Iku. Oya is the bringer of life while Iku is the bringer of death. Guess what? He answered. He said he would grant me my request as long as I did what he asked. And I did what he asked. I gave fake medication so he could manipulate vulnerable minds like yourself."

I couldn't believe the plausibility of that kind of statement. This was the twenty-first century for crying out loud, but she was changing, morphing, swirling. Her hands got larger and her nails turned black.

"But he never gave me back what I wanted," she continued. I clasped my pocket tightly.

"He wanted a trade. That Amaka girl for my baby. I never understood his obsession with her, but I obeyed. I gave him access to Yetunde's body and the rest, they say, is history. I was on my way out for a pregnancy test. It turns out that Iku cannot control life, but he can control death so he did what a god of death would do best. He transferred Yetunde's dead baby into me. Oops, I think I have said too much."

She lifted the syringe in the air and tapped the needle. The fluid trickled down the barrel and I could see the Iku's reflection through it. It was dark and powerful, it laughed, and its voice came out of Dr. Ajayi's lips.

"I like you, dear. I do, so I am just going to give you a little something to help you forget. You do the math, if you run outside, you'll be the case that went rogue, if they don't see me outside, you incriminate yourself, let me just help you forget, so you don't have to remember."

She was about to inject my thigh when a gunshot rented the air and I felt a warm splash on my face. Dr. Ajayi slumped to the ground with the syringe still in hand. I could see blurred figures coming into the living room. I heard Inspector Baba-jide ordering his men to restrain her and take me to the hospital. As I blacked out, I could hear Ahmed calling my name.

Chapter Fifteen

AMAKA

I was released after a week in detention mainly because they had issues with my documentation. A week was more than enough in my opinion. As I left the cell, I said goodbye to all the new friends I made and bought everyone doughnuts. I felt surprised when Inspector Babajide called me to say that they had the real perpetrator and it was Dr. Ajayi. I carried my bag and handed it to Inspector Babajide; Babs, as we, the new prisoners, fondly called him, and he put it in the booth. I entered the front seat and we drove back to school.

"Ahmed proposed to Demola," Inspector Babajide said as we drove. I looked at him and smiled, we had a wedding to plan. He said that Dr. Ajayi was using hallucinatory drugs on us, scopolamine or thereabout. That informed why we forgot things. He said he was not sure of the validity of there being an actual Iku. I felt better recently and I had not had any nightmares. Inspector Babajide requested a toxicology report of the weed I smoked and it showed cocaine, crystal meth and several other hallucinogens mixed with Yetunde's weed. I always carried a batch to Efa because I didn't trust any other source and it was damn too good for its own good. Inyene confirmed that Yetunde had given him a huge stash of weed, too. I always wondered how she got such a huge amount of it, but with everything we know now, the answer was crystal. Inyene was being fed fake drugs and that was why he never saw any improvement whether he took drugs or not. This made us wonder if we were ever really sane in all our transactions if what happened in our heads was what happened.

I thought about Mama and how she didn't need to die. I cried so hard when I found out about her. I didn't eat for days because I was scared that all the food would taste like her food. I thought about Ozioma and how we would handle the funeral. Inspector Babajide was able to confirm Dr. Ajayi's prints from her dead body as well. He said that he could help me cremate her body if I wanted but after giving it some thought, I knew mama wouldn't want that. She would have wanted to be buried in the Christian way.

Yetunde's parents had to come back from the United States themselves to bury her. Her mom was just like her, spirited, curvy and beautiful. She was a mess when I saw her talking to the Inspector. Her dad seemed cold and aloof, a dark contrast against his wife. He had a proud head of dreadlocks. They both looked like hippies, maybe that's why they were never here. Inspector Babajide had given them the papers and told them what they needed to know about her case. I quietly answered all the questions her mother asked.

"Was she happy?" she asked. I didn't know if I should be honest or just tell them that I didn't know.

"Yes, ma," I had said. She gave me a look of gratitude and I knew I had done the right thing. So much had happened in such a short period, I was exhausted and just wanted to rest. I wanted it all to end. Dr. Ajayi's license got revoked by the Medical and Dental Council. She faced prosecution and I was certain that she would not be leaving prison anytime soon. When she got arrested, many of her other patients spoke out about her experimentation and how she would threaten them with her specialist authority status. When I asked her why she killed Mama, she laughed and said, "Why not?"

Seeing Inyene again fulfilled an ache of longing. He was in mufti, jeans and a top with a facecap. He held onto me tightly when he saw me. We visited Ahmed and Demola who were fine and so in love. Demola flashed me her engagement ring while beaming with happiness. I wondered how she was going to be married while still in medical school. I wondered how she and Ahmed planned on doing it, but they planned to transfer to a school outside of Nigeria and start over. Babs and Rita okayed it so Ahmed was home free. Tragedies seem to remind us that we only have a short time here and I was glad Ahmed decided to use his time well.

Inyene went on a walk with me, we walked on the Mushin roads and watched amusingly as some children struggled to get the handkerchief they sold across to us. This time, I just smiled and paid them off. Inyene looked at me with disbelief.

"You didn't need to do that," he said.

"I feel like I had to," I replied. We continued silently, basking in each other's presence, enjoying the moment. He tried to use another route to avoid the uncompleted building, but I decided against it. I wanted to see it. The building was still standing when we got there, a bulldozer beside it ready to demolish it.

"Do you want to watch this?" Inyene asked.

I nodded, watching the breakdown of the building was the most beautiful thing in the world. The walls came crumbling down brick by brick as the building became leveled ground. Inyene watched with me, calmly. I wondered how he was feeling. We had not spoken about that day, what he had to go through and how he managed to find out that Dr. Ajayi was responsible for everything.

"How are you?" I asked him.

"I'm okay," he said, taking my hands in his.

"Are we going to Efa next?" I asked.

"I quit smoking."

We both laughed. We had to because I did, too. I didn't need to ask why I knew. We both knew. This was a new thing, a new start and we wanted to be ready.

"I love you," I said. He turned his face to me, took my face in his hands and kissed me. I kissed him back.

EPILOGUE

I got back home rather slate and went straight to the kitchen. The fridge was wide-open and I went to close it.

"I thought you would never come back today," Ozioma said. She was seated in the dark on the dining table. She stood up and walked over to the fridge. As she tried to close it, an eyeball fell to the floor. I picked it up and placed it back inside.

"You need to be more careful about how you put these things," I said. My blue eyes flashing at her. She bowed, "It won't happen again, master."

"It had better not," I replied. I had worked too hard to get this body and I intended to have as much fun with it as possible. I grabbed a heart from the fridge and dug in.

FINIS

A NOTE ON THE TEXT

The text of this book is set in Minion 3, an updated and expanded version of Robert Slimbach's iconic text typeface. The first version of Minion was released in 1990 and is inspired by classical, old style typefaces of the late Renaissance, a period of elegant, beautiful, and highly readable type designs. Minion Pro combines the aesthetic and functional qualities that make text type highly readable with the versatility of OpenType digital technology, yielding unprecedented flexibility and typographic control, whether for lengthy text or display settings.

Robert Slimbach, who joined Adobe in 1987, began working seriously on type and calligraphy four years earlier in the type drawing department of Autologic in Newbury Park, California. Since then, he has concentrated primarily on designing text faces for digital technology, drawing inspiration from classical sources. In 1991, he received the Prix Charles Peignot from Association Typographique Internationale for excellence in type design. Slimbach now directs Adobe's type design program.

The story titles and subheadings of this book are set in Manofa, designed by Mariya Lish for Inhouse Type foundry. It is inspired by Warren Chappell's Lydian and originated from the experiments with the shape and form of the letter "O". The result is a contemporary, sharp and sculptural display.

Composed by Clever Crow Consulting and Design
Pittsburgh, Pennsylvania

ABOUT THE AUTHOR

Chinaza Eziaghighala is a medical doctor and interdisciplinary writer at the nexus of health, film, and literature, evident in her certifications from the University of Lagos College of Medicine for her Bachelor in Medicine and Bachelor in Surgery degrees (MB; BS); the University of Iowa International Writing Program for Creative Writing in Healthcare; Voodoonauts Fellowship for Black Speculative Fiction Writers, and EbonyLife Creative Academy for Film.

She loves to tell stories based on whatever she finds interesting at the time especially stories that encourage people to both think and feel as they experience the human condition through her eyes. As at when she was writing *Chimera,* she was interested in the intersection of mental illness and African spirituality in a modern day setting. All in all, she loves speculative fiction.

Her short fiction is in British Science Fiction Association's (BSFA) *Fission #2 Vol 1* Anthology, *Mythaxis, Planet Scumm, Metastellar, Future Fiction, BrittlePaper, Afritondo, Please See Me,* Hellboundbooks and BSFA's *Focus.*

She won the 2021 Twelve Days of Brittle Paper Flash Fiction competition for her story "Mmanwu Festival", the 2022 Horror Writers Association Diversity Grant, and the 2022 Young Writers and Creatives Award for "Young Short Story Writer of the Year 2022." Her short story, *Osimiri,* got an Honourable mention in the *Year's Best African Speculative Fiction* Anthology 2022.

She is co-editing the *Year's Best African Speculative Fiction Vol 3.*

A believer in the power of communities, she is a member of the Science Fiction Writers Association, African Speculative Fiction Society, Codex, and the Horror Writers Association.

Due to her passion for television and cinema, she wrote on Africa Magic Viewers' Choice Award-Nominated telenovelas *Itura* and *Masquerades of Aniedo.* She is a Film Development Executive with Jungle Film Works. She also co-wrote and directed a short film for Scriptathon Productions, *The Call,* available on YouTube.

ACKNOWLEDGMENTS

To Dad and Mom, for allowing me write for that 1 year 3 month break after medical school even though we fought consistently when I said I wanted to stop being a doctor for a bit. Thank you for understanding and allowing me to explore this part of myself.

To brother, Iheanyi, for reading the second draft. He said it's a really great story and he never reads anything. This made me glad because this book is meant for people who don't read to start at least. To my other siblings, Chinonso, Kosi, Amazing Grace, for believing that anything I touch turns to gold. Thanks for making your big sister feel like she can take over the world.

To Drs Ibikunle and Richard for beta reading and giving me honest, even, painful feedback. Thanks for also helping me fact check the plausibility of the medical aspects of the book so I at least I know I won't be put to shame, I hope. Lol. Thank you for enjoying the story. It gave me courage to go ahead with publishing.

To Femi Morgan for editing the first draft of the book and helping me identify loopholes in my writing. I've become much better because of your final note.

To Mr Kunle Adewale for encouraging me to write regardless of being a doctor. Arts in Medicine was an important blooming ground for what I would eventually become.

To Ema Uboh who supported me through the writing process. From disagreeing with my using his brother's name to being an excellent emotional pillar at the time. Daalu.

To David and Christine for taking a chance on me. I am eternally grateful.

NOSETOUCH PRESS

Nosetouch Press is an independent book publisher
tandemly based in Chicago and Pittsburgh.
We are dedicated to bringing some of today's most
energizing fiction to readers around the world.

Our commitment to classic book design in a digital
environment brings an innovative and authentic
approach to the traditions of literary excellence.

*We're Out There™

NOSETOUCHPRESS.COM

Horror | Science Fiction | Fantasy | Mystery
Supernatural | Gothic | Weird